Ricky

& other love stories

Whitney Collins

Sarabande Books

Louisville, Kentucky

Publisher's Cataloging-In-Publication Data
(Provided by Cassidy Cataloguing Services, Inc.).

Names: Collins, Whitney, MFA, author.
Title: Ricky & other love stories / Whitney Collins.
Other titles: Ricky and other love stories
Description: First edition. | Louisville, Kentucky : Sarabande Books, [2024]
Identifiers: ISBN: 978-1-956046-23-6 (paperback) | 978-1-956046-24-3 (ebook)
Subjects: LCSH: Love--Fiction. | Women--Fiction. | LCGFT: Short stories. | Magic
realist fiction. | BISAC: FICTION / Short Stories (single author) | FICTION /
Magical Realism. | FICTION / Action & Adventure. | FICTION / Women.
Classification: LCC: PS3603.O45633 R53 2024 | DDC: 813/.6--dc23

Cover and interior by Danika Isdahl.

Printed in USA.
This book is printed on acid-free paper.
Sarabande Books is a nonprofit literary organization.

This project is supported in part by an award
from the National Endowment for the Arts.

for my sister, my sisters

Contents

3   Red Flags

11   Rocks 4 Sale

21   Wild Child

35   The Joneses

43   Ricky

47   Cray

55   Dawn

69   Nine Dreams about Marriage

89   Love Blue

99   I'm Your Venus

113   Ingrid

127   The Yardstick

143   Beans

155   Threesome

163   Petal

169   The Wind

179   Brain, Brian

183   The Owner

189   North Colorado

207   Faster

213   Lush

223   The Split

227   April

Acknowledgments

We have been shark to one another, but also lifeboat.

—Margaret Atwood, *Cat's Eye*

Ricky

&

other love stories

Red Flags

The first thing Ilona saw when she got to the beach was the man, bleeding from his leg with a crowd of people around him. She was far up and away in Phil's condominium, looking down at him from the master bedroom window with her two suitcases in her hands. The man held out his bleeding leg for everyone to admire. Half of the crowd looked down at the leg, half looked out at the ocean. After a minute, the man spread his arms out wide as if to show everyone how much he loved them. *Thissssss much.*

"It faces the beach, see? Just like I promised." Phil came up behind Ilona and palmed her breasts. "What a view, huh?" But Phil wasn't looking at the view. He had his short face in Ilona's long neck and was missing out on the man and the leg and the crowd, which was just fine by Ilona. When Phil went out into the condominium's kitchen, to show her sons some sort of fishing contraption, Ilona went right up to the window, still holding her luggage, and kissed the glass. She had been darkly depressed about herself and her life the whole trip down, and then the man with the bleeding leg appeared and something lightened in her. There was still some good in the world.

The first night, Ilona pretended to sleep in the guest room, to set a good example, but when she could hear her sons breathing deeply from the adjacent room and knew they were asleep, she went into the master bedroom and got into bed with Phil. She had accepted Phil's proposal mostly—no, *entirely*—because she was penniless. Her husband had drunk himself to death because of the debt, and all she was was a speech therapist. How was she to pay for her youngest's lung medication, much less electricity and soup? It only made sense to sleep with someone like Phil, even if the new ring lay on her finger like a lead bullet.

Ilona got under the cold sheets and let Phil root around on her while she squeezed her eyes together and thought about the man with the bleeding leg. This time, Ilona was down at the beach and the man was right in front of her, lifting his leg up just for her to see. The blood ran from his knee to his ankle, and Ilona bent over and licked the man from ankle to knee. Then she straddled his leg and pushed against him, riding up the length of his leg until she was at his waist and he was inside of her. Ilona heard herself gasp, then scream, then the man put his hand over her mouth and dragged her into the ocean. He kept Ilona underwater until she could be quiet for good.

When Ilona woke up, it was three in the morning. She got up from Phil's bed and went back to the guest room where she could not sleep. She lay awake until dawn, thinking of all the terrible mistakes she had ever made. Once, after her youngest had been in the hospital for a week on a ventilator, she had come home to shower and had gotten angry, very angry, at her oldest. It had been about shoes or laundry or money, and she'd slapped him across the chin so hard she could hear his teeth clap together like two plates. Ilona could still see the look on his face. It were as if she'd told him she wished she'd never had him. Had she said that? Maybe she had. What difference did it make? The damage was the same. Ilona rolled over, overcome with love for her sons and hatred for herself, and cried face down in a pillow that Phil's first wife had likely bought. Ilona wept off and on until she heard Phil up making coffee, then she willed herself to rise lest Phil take the boys fishing in some boat without her and her sons were drowned and she was never able to touch them again.

Later that afternoon, Ilona and her sons followed Phil down to the beach, where, with some difficulty, he put up a sun tent and unfolded four chairs. Ilona noticed he was quiet for a time after these efforts, to the extent that she wondered if he might have a secret violent streak. She began to imagine what her future held once the formalities wore off. They didn't know each other all that well. They'd been set up by bored mutual friends desperate for excitement. On the first date, both Phil and Ilona drank heavily. At one point, late in the night, they'd grown teary over their pasts, their presents, their futures. There had been sex on Phil's couch, then embarrassment. The second date had been more proper. The third, dull. Now, in two days, they were going to be married in a courthouse surrounded by palm trees. Phil had brought a yellow suit and Ilona a navy dress. The boys had

5

matching neckties and white suede shoes. Ilona had decided to carry a single tiger lily. Afterward, they would have brunch in a hotel lobby where Ilona would be the only one to order champagne. While everyone ate in silence, Ilona would think about the hotel's beds, the mattresses, the people on them, not sleeping. At that thought, Ilona heard shouting, some sort of commotion further down the beach.

"Someone's bleeding," her oldest said.

"Where?" her youngest asked. "Where, where?"

The victim this time was a woman. And she, too, stood in a crowd of people and lifted up her leg for all to see. The damage appeared to be minor and coming from her heel, but an ambulance was called regardless, and the workers came and bandaged her up, right there on the sand. Then the ambulance drove away empty. Ilona watched the lifeguards put up two red flags, indicating the beach was closed. Ilona's sons went down to the crowd, to meet the lady and ask her questions.

"The sharks are always here," Phil said, his face florid, his thick white hair upright in the breeze. "It's the ocean, you know. It's where they *live*." Ilona squinted out at the horizon, then worked her eyes back toward the shore, looking for a sign—a triangle, a mad tail. Phil went on. "Only fools go swimming past their waist this time of year. Idiots and fools."

Ilona could sense he was still mad about the tent and the chairs, which meant he wasn't mad about the tent and chairs at all. She suspected it was her sons. What use did he have for them? She knew the truth. All he wanted was sex without the children, and all she wanted was money without the sex. It was an age-old transaction, biblical really, but it never sat well. Sooner or later, it led to bad things. Without love, it was hard to keep opening one's wallet or one's legs. Something usually gave. At best, depression and pills took over. At worst? A woman got beaten, a man got poisoned, the law intervened. But what choice did they have? Phil didn't want to die alone, and Ilona didn't want her youngest to die at all.

Down the beach, the crowd scattered. Ilona thought of the man with the bleeding leg and the woman with the bleeding foot. She imagined them interviewed together on the local news. She thought of what they had in common, of how they could make a brave life together. Then she saw her sons running back toward her, smiling, and she thought she might burst from sorrow. If she died, it would be Phil, with his short face and expensive fishing rod, who was left to care for them. It was a thought that made the least sense of any thought Ilona had ever had.

"It was a spinner shark," the oldest said. He was tall and healthy and tan. His name was Leo—a lion, a hero. He would move far away from all of this and have a happy life. "They're mating and angry right now."

"Yes . . ." Her youngest gasped for air. "No one . . . should . . . swim."

Ilona scrambled through her beach bag for the inhaler and reached out for her youngest. He came and curled in her lap and she curled around him. Unlike his brother, he was small and ill and fair. His name was Lester, but everyone called him Les. Ilona felt she had marked him with his name. Still, she feared that he, too, would go far away and have a happy life, except it would be by going to heaven. Ilona hunched over him, humming a tuneless tune with her eyes closed, until he could breathe and she hardly could.

*

That night, Ilona waited for the boys to fall asleep again, then she went into the kitchen and poured herself a glass of warm vodka. She stood in the kitchen facing the refrigerator while she drank. Under a magnet was a recipe for crab cakes written in a woman's cursive. *2 LG eggs*, Ilona read. *3tbs mayo—DUKE'S BRAND ONLY!!!* Phil's first wife looked something like Carly Simon. Ilona had seen a picture or two. She had a big mouth full of big teeth. She looked full of confidence and opinions. "She was always happy," Phil had explained. "Just not with me."

Ilona finished the vodka and went into the master bedroom. Like the rest of the condominium, it was air-conditioned and sterile—all chrome and Lucite. Phil was propped up in bed reading a magazine with a sailfish on the front. He had on little reading glasses and no shirt. Ilona looked at his drooping chest and the white hairs around his nipples. Her mood lifted when she let herself realize he had less life left in him every day.

"Is the beach everything you thought it would be?" Phil asked.

Ilona went and turned off one lamp and then the other. She was not there for conversation. She was there to put him to sleep. "Yes," she said, kneeling at the edge of the bed. She did not want him inside her tonight. "It is."

Ilona did her thing and Phil did his, and when he was breathing low and steady, Ilona went out to the kitchen and poured herself another glass of vodka, which she used to rinse her mouth. In the boys' room, she lay slender and motionless, first next to her oldest, then next to her youngest. Once again, she could not sleep, but instead of thinking of things she'd done wrong, she thought of the sharks, mating and angry, still out there in the black night and the black sea, flashing back and forth, silver against silver, a world of knife fights. She thought of money, too, of how much it took to stay alive, and how those who had it used it to catch those who didn't. She saw Phil and his fishing rod, money on the end of the hook, the hook in her hand. She rolled over and spooned her youngest and placed her palm slowly on his chest. His lungs were working hard to keep him alive. If he died, Ilona would, too, and in that sense, his two weak lungs were responsible for keeping two people on the earth. "Thank you," Ilona whispered. "Thank you thank you thank you."

At some point, Ilona fell asleep. At some point, she jerked awake. In between, she had a dream—a thin one she could not recall. It went through her brain like a band of smoke, and then it was gone. For a moment, Ilona knew what the beach had once been like, before the people had come with their chrome and Lucite. She saw tangles of green vines, snakes and panthers, the skulls of doomed humans crushed by the smiles of armored alligators. People used to have less hope, less luck. Dying had not been so unreasonable. Ilona sat up quietly then went to the window. Between the black sky and black water, there was a growing orange, like a giant eye opening up. Ilona stood there while the morning took over the night. Eventually, in the great pink light, she was able to see something—*someone*—walking across the dunes and toward the ocean. The silhouette was slow-moving in the soft sand, but once it reached the wide expanse of hard shore, it picked up speed and ran—straight into the surf. Ilona leaned forward until her lips almost touched the glass. She squeezed her eyes together and saw: it was Phil—ankle-deep, knee-deep, waist-deep, shoulders. He went out into the ocean until he was just a head, bobbing. And then he went under and came back up, and then under again. Ilona watched, breathless. While she waited, her heart leapt and quickened in a way she had not expected.

Rocks 4 Sale

Every morning at 8:30, Ursula came shuffling out of her house in her red bathrobe carrying her box of rocks. The rocks were in the flimsy top half of an old doughnut box that sagged toward its front as Ursula walked across the lawn, indicating the rocks had slid forward and were close to tumbling out. Even still, Ursula always made it to the card table without losing a rock. She was good—or lucky—like that.

Once the box was on the table and Ursula was in her lawn chair, she treated herself to her first generic menthol of the day. She smoked in an unapologetic and professional way, blowing perfect, bored Os and tapping out the butt on the card table's rusted leg when she'd had enough. Afterward, Ursula got up out of her lawn chair and shuffled to the front of the table and taped up her sign. The sign said: *ROCKS 4 SALE. $4 EACH.* The rocks were nothing more than pieces of ordinary gravel, the chalky kind found near the fringes of new blacktop, and all of them were more or less the size of tater tots. Sometimes, in the process of setting up shop, one of Ursula's long breasts fell out of her robe. If one did, she just let it hang there while she finished doing whatever it was she was doing. Shame was not in Ursula's vocabulary.

Every morning at 8:29, Brownie stood at her kitchen window, holding off on coffee and urination until she'd seen what she had dubbed the Ursula Rock Concert. She loved Ursula. Not her body or brains, because she didn't have much of either, but her faith and determination. Somewhere around 9:00, after Maxwell House and the toilet, but before she started in on the bourbon, Brownie joined Ursula at the card table. She had to bring her own chair. She had to initiate conversation. Ursula never looked Brownie in the eye—not when she unfolded her chair and not when she turned to face her. This was another thing that stole Brownie's heart: Ursula's disinterest and independence. Her ease with detachment.

"We need rain," Brownie said.

"Nah," Ursula replied, staring out at their dull street, Acorn Lane. "What for?"

Brownie felt dumb even though it was Ursula's reply that made no sense. "For the farmers," she said. "For the grass. See here?" She pointed. "It's nearly turned silver with thirst."

Ursula did not consider the grass, only a house across the road—an ancient, run-down Sears Catalog Home the color of snot. "Let it, then," she said. "Let us all burn up and shrivel. What's the fuss about?"

Brownie thought about this, which made her also think about bourbon.

"So, we die. Then what?" Ursula shrugged. "Maybe we feed the worms and that's it. Lights out, worm food. Or maybe we go to heaven or maybe we go to hell or maybe we float around in outer space and bang our heads on some stars." Ursula leaned forward and gave the old doughnut box a little shake back and forth as if sifting sand. Brownie wondered if she thought this might attract a customer. "What difference does it make? Whatever happens, happens. We're all on the train going full steam ahead. There's no getting off."

Brownie felt a low, slow terror at this thought, but also a deep admiration for Ursula; she was fearless. Brownie saw her on a runaway train, floating in space, on a cloud, in the dirt, engulfed in flames, and in every instance the look on her face was the same: stony, glacial. Almost serene.

Acorn Lane ran through a neighborhood that had once, in the '70s and '80s, belonged to white, penny-pinching retirees. Shriners and knitters. Librarians and organists. Then in the '90s, when all the retirees died and all the houses started to lean and fade, the neighborhood shifted to people like Brownie and Ursula—sad-faced, mostly fortysomethings with a range of addictions and afflictions, some active, some dormant. Acorn Lane people were people who had long ago given up on true love and music careers. They were broken and broke and needed cheap houses over apartments, because they all had big or suspicious dogs—Great Danes and pits—that kept them from not just relapse and despair and seizures, but renting. And most of them were on disability like Brownie (her heart) and Ursula (her spine).

"You think anyone from Acorn Lane ever made anything of themselves?" Brownie asked Ursula one day. "Like with a hit song or the Lotto?"

Ursula shook her box of rocks. "What does 'make something of yourself' even mean? Someone writes a song and gets paid to sing it over and over and over. What? You go out on the road for the rest of your life and sit in motels trying to write another song but this one has to be better? What a trap."

Brownie didn't know what to say.

"The Lotto," Ursula said. Her hair was dyed matte black like an old, spray-painted car. "What does the Lotto get you? A new refrigerator? A dishwasher? Some shoes? Some more shoes? A closet for the shoes? A closet for the closet?" A car passed and Ursula shook the box again. "All that's happening when someone goes from this neighborhood to that neighborhood is movement. Someone on the train is getting up out of their seat and going to another train car. Maybe the cocktail car. Maybe the dining car. Maybe a car that is identical to the one they were just sitting in. The people are getting up out of their seats and sitting in other seats, but guess what?"

Brownie shook her head.

"Those assholes are still on the train." Ursula lit up a menthol. "Choo-choo," she said without emotion. "Chugga-chugga."

Ursula stared blankly at the silver lawn. Brownie watched Ursula smoke. Ursula was a goddess. Ursula was a god—The God. Brownie thought she might cry. Brownie felt like she might explode. Brownie prayed to Ursula right then and there in her head. *Dear Ursula,* the prayer went. *Please love me. Do you love me? Please love me. Amen.*

One day Ursula was late. Brownie was not. She was at her window at 8:29 and when Ursula didn't appear at 8:30 or 8:31 or 8:32,

Brownie broke out in a cold sweat. She got the shakes. Her first thought was that Ursula was dead inside her little blue house. How would Brownie get in? Did she leave it open? Was it locked with a deadbolt? Would Brownie have to throw her lawn chair through her dark front window and climb over glass shards to find her on the floor and touch her neck for a pulse? Did Brownie even know how to find a pulse? Would she? Could she? Brownie was a wreck.

And then, Ursula came out. At 8:36, Ursula came shuffling out in her red robe with the flimsy box. Brownie thanked God. She thanked Ursula. She gripped the kitchen sink and watched her set up shop. Brownie went without her coffee. She didn't use the bathroom. She had a bourbon ahead of schedule. *What would she do without Ursula if something really did happen?* she wondered. At 8:52, Brownie could not control herself any longer. She went out early with her lawn chair and sat next to Ursula.

"I thought you might have taken a trip out of town," Brownie said. "When I didn't see you and all." Brownie looked at Ursula and Ursula looked different. Her eyes were puffed up like she'd been thinking sad thoughts, but Brownie knew Ursula didn't do that. "The pollen's something else today," Brownie said. "Shoo-wee. I can feel it in my throat. I can feel it in my eyes."

Ursula didn't say anything. One of her breasts had escaped her robe. She sat in her lawn chair and let her breast do its thing in the sunlight, hanging like a pale stocking. Brownie tried not to look at it, but she did. It was made of tender skin, not weathered skin like Ursula's face. The nipple on it was the color of ham and pointed toward the silver lawn.

"Today's the day," Ursula said after some time. "I can feel it."

Brownie pretended she hadn't been looking at Ursula's breast.

She pretended she knew what Ursula meant. She looked across the street at the dismal houses. She couldn't have told the police who lived in any of them if someone'd come knocking to ask.

"Today's the day for rain?" Brownie finally said.

"Nope," Ursula said, sitting forward to shake the box of rocks. "Not that."

Ursula tucked in her breast and retied the belt of her robe. Then she lit a cigarette and blew out a perfect O. Brownie looked at Ursula's rocks and counted them in her head. There were twenty-seven in total. Brownie wanted to know what Ursula meant—*Today's the day*—but she was just like God, all-knowing and no hints. The suspense was both terrific and terrible. Brownie and Ursula sat in silence together all morning.

At lunchtime, Brownie went inside. She stood at her kitchen sink and drank a bourbon and ate some cold beans straight from a can and watched Ursula. When the limousine rattled by, she was on her third bourbon. The limousine was gold and dented and needed a muffler, but still: it was a real limousine right there on Acorn Lane. It drove past loud and slow going west and Ursula didn't flinch. A minute later it was back, still moving loud and slow but now pointing east. It came to a stop in front of Ursula's house. A rear window on the limousine went down. Brownie couldn't see inside the car. She heard a voice call out, like a small dog barking, but she couldn't understand what it said. Brownie watched; Ursula's mouth didn't move, but Brownie saw her shake her head. Then Brownie saw her get up and shuffle to the front of the card table where she pointed at her sign. One of her breasts fell out and she shuffled back around to her lawn chair and her breast slid back in. That was when the man emerged from the limousine. He was in a bright blue suit, the color of a good day,

16

and he strode right up to the table and dipped his head in a kind of a bow. Brownie watched the man point a finger over the rocks, counting them, it seemed, just as Brownie had. Then the man reached into his back pocket and pulled out a wallet and pulled out a stack of bills and counted out nine or ten of them and gave them to Ursula. Following that, the man reached for the box of rocks and Ursula nodded. Brownie watched as the man walked back to the limousine with the box of rocks. When the man got to the car, he didn't open the door. He just tipped the rocks into the limousine's open window. Then he opened the door and climbed in and the window went back up. Then the limousine drove off, loud and slow.

Brownie felt as though she'd watched a crime occur. A kidnapping, a theft. A murder, even. She set her glass down on the edge of the sink. She went, unnerved, to her front door. By the time she made it across her silver lawn and over to Ursula's yard, Ursula had already folded up her lawn chair and taken down the sign. The card table was flipped over on its top and Ursula was having some trouble folding in its rusted legs.

"Did you just sell all the rocks?"

Ursula grunted as the first leg folded inward. She promptly got to work on the second. "Don't you remember?" she said. "I told you today was the day."

Brownie could see the wad of cash in the front pocket of Ursula's robe. Both of her breasts were out and swaying as she got to work on the table's third leg. "How did you know?" Brownie said. "How did you know today was the day?"

Bent over, Ursula's hair parted in such a way to show an inch of new silver growth. It was a silver that put the grass to shame. "The train never stops," Ursula said. "But sometimes, real quick, it passes by something you were hoping to see."

Ursula folded the final leg inward on the table. Then, with her breasts loose and her hair loose and the rest of her red bathrobe opening up to shamelessly show all of herself, both the weathered and the tender, Ursula put the table under one arm and the sign between her front teeth and the chair under her other arm. Then she shuffled back inside her house and closed her door.

After that, Ursula didn't come out anymore. The Ursula Rock Concert was canceled. Brownie stood at her kitchen window every morning and watched and waited and wept, but Ursula didn't come out at 8:30 or 8:31 or 2:47 or 6:55. Brownie drank and slept, drank and slept. She had dreams she was on a train. The train didn't have windows. No one would tell her where they were going.

One day, Brownie looked out the window and saw: something had been put on the curb in front of Ursula's house. Brownie stood there squinting until she determined it was Ursula's old lawn chair. Brownie staggered out of her house and over to Ursula's curb and stole the chair for herself. She brought it right into Ursula's front yard and unfolded it so that it was facing Ursula's front door. Then Brownie went back into her house and got her own lawn chair. She took it back to Ursula's front lawn and unfolded it right next to the first chair. Brownie took a seat. She stared at Ursula's front door. Up above, the sky was a pale gray that fell somewhere between the color of the old grass and Ursula's new hair. Brownie closed her eyes. After some time, she could hear it. *Choo-choo. Chugga-chugga.* It was the train and she was on it and it was moving fast. Brownie opened her eyes again. She stared at Ursula's door. She would sit there as long as it took.

She'd sit there in the day and in the night. She'd sit there when it was warm and when it was cold. She'd even sit there if it rained, which that day, it finally did.

Wild Child

*W*hen *Imogen logs* on to the sperm bank's website, she sees that it will not be like ordering a salad. With a salad she can say, "Whoa, now! Easy on the chickpeas," or "Hold the croutons," or "Let's do green goddess instead of raspberry vinaigrette." But at the sperm bank, the menu is prix fixe, not à la carte. At the sperm bank, it's: *No substitutions, please.* With anonymous ejaculate, it's a package deal.

For example, Imogen likes hazel eyes but not lawyers, and yet here is Donor AX45TR8, a hazel-eyed lawyer. Imogen likes not-too-tall classical musicians, but lo and behold here is TH72HS9: a lovely five-niner who has the audacity to have mastered the electric guitar. Imogen must prioritize. What is most important? IQ or EQ? Fingernails with half-moons or earlobes that are attached? Yale or hale? Perfect pitch or someone who has pitched a perfect game?

What Imogen wants is this: a doe-eyed son with an inde-fatigable zest for life. A boy skilled in listening and wit. Social justice and socializing. An animal lover, a cellist, a champion swimmer. *The butterfly.*

Don't get her wrong. It's not that Imogen seeks perfection. Perfect people are friendless people; she would know. It's just that minimally flawed humans have an easier time in the world, and who doesn't want ease for their offspring? Go on, Imogen nods to the laboratory gods. Give the child an imperfection, but have the defect be the sort of blemish that imbues humility and exudes affability: a birthmark in the shape of Hawaii, a space between the front teeth, hay fever.

The last thing Imogen wants is craziness or laziness. Can a professional in the field of semen tell her more about the thrill-seeking gene or hereditary narcolepsy? Can someone promise that her child will not make derelict decisions or fall asleep at the opera? Can she pay more for these sorts of guaran-tees? Because Imogen has stocks and bonds and platinum cards with her name on them. Imogen has been saving for a long time for the child who will save her.

Imogen studies the donors. She imagines their frozen sperm. Way in the back of some sterile office, there are test tubes filled with arctic tadpoles that will thaw inside of Imogen. They will race to meet her pale and reticent egg. One tadpole will prevail and grow into a frog and this frog will grow inside of Imogen until it emerges as frogs do: from the darkness, in the springtime, wet and blinking, its voice new and untested. She will hold this frog and wipe it clean and then she will kiss it. Her kiss will turn the frog into a prince. *Her* prince. She will name him something royal. Rex, Duke, Earl, Laird.

Imogen decides on GU39QP1. Her virtual baby daddy. He's a teal-eyed veterinarian. He plays the oboe. He was, *is*—he's out there, somewhere, calling cats instead of catcalling—proficient at pickleball and Mandarin and crosswords and sign language, though rest assured he is not deaf, nor is anyone in his gene pool. He has no family history of anything other than color blindness, to which Imogen thinks: *A world, muted, is not such a bad thing.*

Imogen clicks, the sperm will be shipped, her doctor will be picked. When her monthly egg is on the verge of dropping into the proverbial straw, Donor GU39QP1 will rush to meet it. Just like in baggage claim, he will be a man with a sign, searching and hopeful. Her egg, a woman laden with both luggage and longing. Imogen has never known love; it is the only thing she has ever wanted. Unable to find it beyond herself, she will cultivate it within herself. She is a farmer. The baby is the harvest. She will grow what she seeks.

After Imogen makes her decision, she goes out to lunch. "I'll have a salad," she says to the server. "Easy on the chickpeas. Hold the croutons. Green goddess, please."

Before Imogen can have regrets about the oboe or pickleball, there is a phone call. The sample has arrived at her doctor's. Imogen imagines a white Styrofoam cooler and dry ice, a pair of metal tongs producing a tadpole popsicle from a burst of fog. That night, Imogen's anticipation keeps her from deep sleep; she half dreams of a football field heaving with bullfrogs. She must wade through them to find the one meant for her, the most shiny and emerald one. The one with the tilted golden crown. At dawn, Imogen dresses in a baby-blue skirt and matching blazer. *Laird,* she says over breakfast. *Rex, Duke, Earl.* She decides on Laird. She decides to skip her espresso. She decides at the last minute to shave her privates, one leg then the other propped up near the kitchen sink. She forgoes soap and powder for fear they will kill the sperm.

Laird, she thinks in the taxi. *King Laird.* There is traffic, the ride is long. Her privates burn. Imogen has time to fret. Laird will be difficult for others to spell and pronounce. Laird is not a playground name. Imogen decides instead on Lear with an *e-a,* then Leer with an *e-e,* then Lee, like the American jeans. And also, the American Confederate. Imogen frowns and fumbles for her cab fare. "Rex" rhymes with "sex." "Duke" rhymes with "puke." "Earl" rhymes with "pearl." Earl it will be.

When the doctor injects the sperm, Imogen imagines the teal-eyed veterinarian inside of her, thrusting in a considerate and unselfish way. He offers to take her out afterward for halibut and Manhattans, but Imogen declines, because this is business and she is resolute. *Thanks, but no thanks,* she smiles to herself. *Earl and I got this.* The doctor lets Imogen rest with her feet in the metal stirrups for as long as she likes. She sings "Michael, Row the Boat Ashore" and then falls asleep. She dreams she is covered in lily pads, that she is made of them. When she wakes, Imogen pats her abdomen; three taps on the left ovary, three taps on the right. She lifts each arm and sniffs into each pit; they smell faintly of moss.

The next day, she goes to work like nothing has occurred. Well, maybe a manicure or an eyebrow waxing. A thorough flossing. She takes turns tapping on her keyboard and tapping on her stomach. For lunch, Imogen eats kale and quinoa with a wooden spoon from a wooden bowl. For dinner, she pours an entire bottle of gin down the drain. For twelve consecutive evenings, Imogen walks to the drugstore for fun and gathers sticks like kindling. She brings them back to her apartment and urinates on them, one white twig after another, until, one day, there is a fire: two red flames erupt on a single stick, side by side and bright in the night.

The baby settles in Imogen like a pumpkin seed, at first timorous and tame, sending out its blind, searching tendrils and fumbling like a child down a dark hallway. Imogen drinks organic milk and watches nature documentaries. She rubs her stomach and smiles in a superior way. *Mama, Mama,* she hears the child cry in the night. *I'm right here,* she says. *See?*

A few days pass. The tendrils reach the sides of Imogen's womb. They latch on at first like fireflies to fingertips, and then, rapacious, like mousetraps to thumbs. The tendrils invade her insides, they grow hairy and dark. They turn from bean sprouts to grapevines. They drink of her blood. They drain her of iron and irony.

Before long, Imogen is rendered voiceless by nausea. She takes a leave from work. She resists looking at the sun. She must sip water in the tiniest of sips. She finds her grandmother's silver thimble and drinks from it. Imogen can hardly leave the couch. She can hardly will herself to wash a dish, change a sock. The mail gathers on the floor beneath the brass slot. She pretends the bills are love letters from the laboratory gods. *We are sorry,* the gods write. *You should be,* thinks Imogen. She has food delivered. She eats two bites, leaves the containers on the floor. Cockroaches scatter this way and that. Imogen watches them through one squinted eye. She pretends they are musical notes, dark and bouncing. She tries to sing a lullaby. To herself, not the child.

*

25

At two months, a golden flower bursts within her. Imogen sees it in a dream, then wakes and smells the faint scent of daffodils. At three months, the flower curls into itself like a green nut and Imogen, for the first time in her life, is able to whistle. The nausea subsides. She returns to work. At four months, the nut becomes a gourd. It inflates like a basketball, pumped. Imogen is filled with an inexplicable lightness, a manic merriment. A twinkle returns to her eyes. There is pink in her cheeks. Suddenly, she craves only meat. She buys porterhouses and skirt steaks and lollipop lamb chops from the corner butcher. At night, in the moonlight, she sucks marrow from bones. She saves the bones and puts them in a bucket of bleach. Later, after the baby arrives and while he naps, Imogen will make a chandelier from them. In the meantime, she declutters her apartment. She throws away her diplomas. She gives her gold jewelry to the homeless. She cuts off her hair and puts it in a silk pillowcase. She staples the pillowcase closed and mails it to France. Imogen considers a color for the baby's room. She remembers the baby may be colorblind. She decides on ivory—*rib, calcium, skeleton.*

At the twenty-week ultrasound, the doctor points to a brewing storm on the screen. "It's a boy," he says. "See here."

"Of course it is," Imogen laughs. "What else would it be?" She squints at the screen, where the doctor points, and sees something small and inconsequential. Imogen has a vision of the future. Of a locker room. Of Earl, hardly unfurled.

"He'll have a big personality," the doctor grins. "Larger than life."

Imogen has never had friends, at least none who have lasted longer than a month. She has blamed this on her beauty and her brains, but deep down she knows it is because she is bottomless. She is a booby trap. To engage her is to stumble into a deep canyon disguised by a thin layer of pine straw.

Bart is a new employee at Imogen's firm. He has only been there two weeks; his enthusiasm is still palpable.

"We should have a shower," he says to Imogen at the water cooler. "Is there not going to be a shower for you and the baby?"

Imogen shrugs, but her heart flutters. The baby leaps in a biblical way. The pine straw rustles. "What's your number?" she stammers. "Your phone?"

Bart acts as if he has misheard. He smiles. "I'll organize," he says. "What fun."

On the day of the shower there is a scattering of gift cards on the conference table but only Bart and Imogen in attendance. The office is empty.

"Where is everyone?" Bart is perplexed. "This can't be right."

Imogen peels the blue wrappers from six blue cupcakes and sets them back down, naked on the tray. She is quivering. She does not eat them. She is filled with the thrill of possibly being loved. "What's your address?" she says to Bart. "Where do you live?"

Bart looks at Imogen and eats a cupcake slowly. Imogen imagines Bart wiping her tears, braiding her hair, assembling a tricycle, stirring a stir-fry. Here he is, his arm around her waist. They are picking out towels, picking out a beach house, picking out headstones. Here they stand in a garden of roses, and here is a sword, and here goes Bart falling on it, for her, their son. Who was not his son but now is.

"I have to go," Bart says. There is blue frosting in the corners of his mouth, as if he has suddenly understood something and can no longer attend to basic manners. "Congratulations."

And then, nothing new; Imogen is alone with her gift cards. At home that night she sits in the baby's femur-colored rocker and thinks of her estranged parents, her strange self. She waits for the baby to kick her three times: *I. Love. You.*

Imogen pays someone to be with her in the delivery room. A delivery guy. A literal one. His name is Shawn, from Domino's, and he needs money. Imogen offers him five hundred. Shawn stalls. Imogen offers a grand. Shawn accepts. Imogen pays him three hundred up front and takes her pizza, mushroom. Shawn writes the date on his palm. The birth is scheduled in three weeks, a C-section.

"Rad," Shawn says at the fifteen crisp twenties. "Sweet!"

"It's a boy," Imogen says. She will throw out the pizza when Shawn leaves. "His name is Earl and you can meet him when he is older and pretend to be a cousin, an uncle."

"I can teach him to drive stick," Shawn says.

Imogen sees Shawn at her door in sixteen years. He has a beard. He tousles Earl's tidy crewcut. "Will you hold my hand when they cut me open?" she whispers.

Shawn laughs like a boy, because he is a boy. "For a grand I think I have to."

On the morning of Earl's birth, Imogen drains the bleach from the meat bones and sets them to dry on her dining table. There are enough bones to build an entire cow, minus its skull. The apartment smells of chlorine, a drained pool. Imogen drinks a glass of prosecco in the nude. She fries a cube steak in butter and eats it with a spoon. She puts on a silk robe, baby blue. In the cab, she tells the driver that her husband left her for an infertile redhead named Jennica. The driver tells her he is sorry, and Imogen drinks his pity like a second glass of wine. At registration, Shawn, the delivery boy, is waiting. He wears jeans caked with flour and smells of tomato sauce. Imogen hands him an envelope with fourteen fifties.

"Go and buy me a blue teddy bear in the gift shop," she tells him. "And a blue vase of blue lollipops and a giant blue balloon shaped like a stork."

Shawn nods his head. He trots off in the direction of the gift shop but forty minutes later has still not returned. Imogen knows: he was only there for his money. She proceeds on her own. She puts on her hospital gown. She lets the nurses prep her. They shave her. They swab her abdomen with yellow antiseptic. She lets the nurses look into her sad eyes with their sad eyes, and their concern fills Imogen with joy.

An hour later, when the doctor pulls the baby from Imogen and announces that it's a girl, Imogen pretends he is wrong. She pretends that girl does not rhyme with pearl. She pretends not to see the swollen folds between Earl's legs. She pretends not to notice Earl's narrow shoulders and rosebud mouth. When she holds Earl to her breast and coos, "My son, my prince, my boy!" she pretends the nurses regard her with admiration and not terror. For the four days Imogen is in the hospital, she pretends she is trembling from love and is sleepless from joy.

For a month, Earl is a pearl. Imogen feeds and hums and swaddles. She sleeps in seven-minute intervals. She lives on sugar water and canned sausages. She practices different ways of laughing. Imogen watches the wound below her breasts and above her privates, from which her prince emerged, heal into a shiny pink smile. She talks to herself in French. She composes a national anthem in her head. Earl is the country to which she sings. One day, Imogen feels well enough to take the bones from the dining room table and attempt a chandelier, but she cannot find the glue. She cannot remember what glue looks like. She puts the bones into the metal trash can and begins to cry. Soon after, Earl begins to cry. Before long, Imogen begins to scream. Not to be outdone, Earl follows suit.

Earl and Imogen howl for days. The tenants respond at first by pounding on their floors and ceilings with broomsticks, but then on Imogen's door with fists. Imogen takes the metal trash can of bones and rattles it for an hour until Earl sleeps for an hour. An hour of rattling, an hour of sleep. Over the course of a week, Imogen's biceps grow large, her eyes grow frantic. Scream, shake, sleep. Weep, bang, heap. At last, the landlord arrives. His smile is sheepish. His hat is wadded in his hands. He asks Imogen to temporarily relocate.

"Two months," he says. "The rent is on me."

"A beach vacation?" Imogen says. She repeats it to herself in French. *Des vacances à la plage?* She laughs for the first time in weeks. It flutters to the ceiling like a bird let out of a cage. "How generous!" she says. "How kind!"

"Well, I . . ." the landlord stammers. He looks at his feet. He shuffles his feet. Earl lets loose with a shriek. The child turns the color of Mars. The landlord turns ivory—*rib, calcium, skeleton*. Broomsticks bang overhead and underfoot. "The beach it is," he mumbles. "The beach it is!" he shouts.

Imogen stares at the landlord. His hair is gray at the temples. He looks drained and pained. Imogen sees him in a beach chair with a tropical drink. She sees him beside her, feels him inside her. "Come with me," she says. "Come with us."

The landlord opens and closes his mouth. He fumbles for his wallet. He hands Imogen its contents and backs out of the apartment, flustered. "I have to go," he says. But Imogen hears: *I love you so.*

Imogen packs a suitcase with the bleached bones, the baby-blue robe, the baby-blue suit, her grandmother's thimble. She slides the unused gift cards from her office shower into her wallet like a slick brick. She places Earl in a linen sling printed with gray whales and wears the baby across her body like a pageant sash. For two cab rides and two flights, Earl is uncharacteristically silent. When Imogen arrives at the hotel, she stands in front of it and feels light and elated. She breathes in the sea. She takes in the sun. She marvels at the silence. Earl has nothing to emote until Imogen is in her double queen deluxe, sipping from a pineapple filled with cream and rum and looking out at the ocean, and then Earl unfurls like a tidal wave. Earl's screams crash through Imogen's room and the rooms beyond like a storm surge. By dinnertime, Imogen and Earl are relocated by the management to the highest floor, and the surrounding guests are relocated to the lowest. On the second day, Imogen is sent a complimentary breakfast and three blue pills. On the third day, she is sent away. With free shoehorns and shower caps.

Earl is a relentless, vacation-ruining rain. But still, a second hotel takes Imogen for a night, and a third takes her for an afternoon. A bed-and-breakfast lets a banished and famished Imogen eat her takeout dinner in their parking lot, but at the town's final motel, the staff sees her coming and locks the doors. From the tiny glass lobby, they wave and shrug and hold up a sign that reads: *WE'VE HEARD ABOUT YOU.* "Heard" is painted in bright, furious-baby red.

Imogen wheels her suitcase down to the beach. It digs its heels into the sand, and Imogen pitches forward as if beaten back by a headwind. At the water's edge, she looks left, which is north, and right, which is south, and, craving warmth, decides on south. She staggers past sunbathers and ball-tossers and dogs with their ears pinned flat to their heads. Everyone hears Imogen and Earl coming. Everyone stops for the parade. The spectators' gapes are their salutes. Their silence is their homage. The suitcase's wheel ruts mark the highway to hell, and nothing dares cross over them. Not person or pet, sea-foam or seaweed.

When the day is done and the sky is the color of funeral ash and the bait fish rise and fall like tossed silver coins, Imogen nears a stretch of protected land free from civilization where she can, at last, be uncivilized. She sets Earl down in the sand. Earl writhes and wails in the sling. Imogen opens the suitcase and dumps the bones into a pile, and beside the pile she lays back, ready for outlining, like a gunshot victim. One by one, she takes the bones and pokes them into the sand, tracing herself. She goes around her legs and in between them. She pokes around one arm using one hand to place the bones. Around the other arm using the other hand. When Imogen is done, the bones are a white picket fence and she is the vacant house within.

Imogen sits up and sighs. She stands and tiptoes outside of her perimeter. She gathers the gift cards and presses them into the sand above her picket head, fanned like a liberty crown. She takes the complimentary shoehorns and arranges them into the shape of a sword, a tortoiseshell weapon that begins in her bony hand in the sand and points north, away from a pretend god. As Earl would have it, milk pours from Imogen's breasts the entire time she works. As Imogen would have it, she removes her stained suit at sunset and stands naked. She gathers the free shower caps and sets them out to sea like manmade jellyfish. She releases her suit to the wind, and it lands in the ocean behind the translucent shower caps, a pale-blue polyester ray. Imogen puts on her robe. She puts her grandmother's thimble on her thumb. She puts on the writhing, wailing, whale sling and tiptoes back inside of her bony outline and reclines with Earl on her chest.

The screams fade out as the tide comes in. The sea laps at Imogen's swollen feet, at her veined legs and virgin crotch. It reaches the pink smile on her abdomen, then Earl's back and her chest. The baby turns silent and still. Imogen pats Earl's back with the silver thimble. She hums "Michael, Row the Boat Ashore." She sings an anthem, hears a cello. She sees cockroaches turn into water bugs and water bugs turn into thimbles. Each wave fills a thimble with wet sand, and each thimbleful is dropped into a canyon. As the canyon fills, the birth is rewound in Imogen's mind. Earl shrinks from infant to gourd, from gourd to green nut, from green nut to golden flower to tadpole. Imogen sees a tadpole sucked into a syringe. A popsicle refrozen. She sees a teal-eyed veterinarian who cannot bring himself pleasure holding an empty sample cup. Imogen opens her eyes. In the path of the moonlight, the bones float out to sea, one after another, in the shape of a ladder. A perfect girl climbs one slippery rung at a time, but Imogen pretends not to see her. Imogen closes her eyes. She tastes salt in her mouth, but whether it is seawater or tears, she cannot say.

In the morning, Imogen wakes from a dream in which a

single bone rattles in a metal trash can. When she opens her eyes, she sees her thumb, the silver thimble, tap, tap, tapping on her chest. In place of Earl, there is a breastplate made of pearl. *Mother of pearl.* Imogen rises in her wet, blue robe. She looks north and south for her prince, and then she looks out at the ocean and remembers. A champion swimmer. *The butterfly.*

Imogen packs her empty suitcase with ten thimblefuls of wet sand. Of the three gift cards that remain, she takes one and slides it into the pocket of her robe. She sets off, wheeling further south until she can hear the whine of civilization but not see it. Imogen trudges eastward over sea oats and dunes. Thrice she stops to catch her breath, to tap the silver thimble on her breastplate. Eventually, she emerges in a parking lot. Across a two-lane road, she spies a diner. Imogen proceeds toward and through the cry of traffic. She parks her suitcase at the restaurant's door. She tightens the sash of her robe. Inside the diner, she requests a table for one. Imogen's server narrows his eyes at her as he hands her a menu.

"Would you like to hear you're special?" Imogen thinks she hears him say.

"No," Imogen says, eyes downcast. "I'm good."

Imogen knows she will order a salad. The one with the most ingredients. Croutons and chickpeas. Green goddess and raspberry vinaigrette. Reticent eggs and pickleballs and green nuts and pumpkin seeds.

"One loaded salad," the server will say. "Do you want me to hold anything?"

And Imogen will keep looking down and she will answer *No*, because she knows if she looks up, she will say *Me*.

The Joneses

et me introduce you to the Joneses. You don't know them, but you do. I mean, you haven't met them, but you have.

You might recognize the dad. He sports brown hair with strands of silver, moderate sideburns, size ten driving moccasins. He has a smile like he broke a vase and hid the vase. He is forever, desperately, trying to look like he cares even though he doesn't. Mr. Jones always says things like "Great job, kiddo!" and "Love you, babe," and "Chicken sounds great," when what he means is "When do you move out?" and "Leave me alone," and "A bottle of gin, an Ambien. A box of fudge. Another."

Mr. Jones feels nada. Emotion is a letdown. Caring is such a charade. Speaking of, when Mr. Jones is asked to play charades, he doesn't do anything. He just stands there with his arms at his sides and waits for people to guess the answer. The answer is NOT GIVING A SHIT because he is not giving one.

Here's what's good in Mr. Jones's world: Obliteration! Cirrhosis! Diabetes! So much porn it becomes like watching a dull weather forecast. Partly cloudy, partly cloudy, partly cloudy. To be numb—a human callus—that's the ticket for Mr. Jones! Do you still recognize him? Yes or no? If it helps, he's wearing a vest. It's a fleece one, from Costco. Charcoal gray. His phone case is black. It's the industrial kind of case meant for contractors, but he is not a contractor. Mr. Jones's job isn't worth mentioning. I see you nodding. I see that you see him.

Now. Here we have the wife and mother, Mrs. Jones. Wave hello, because you know her, too! Don't act like you don't. You guys are buds. Mrs. Jones has her hair up and her sleeves up and she looks like she needs a nap. She smells like Bounce dryer sheets and one desperate drag from a Camel Light. Mrs. Jones is always trying to make everyone care as much as she does. Really, to have such a giant heart in this world is so precious, so pathetic. Every day, Mrs. Jones shows up for life with that genuine smile of hers. It's like bringing a butter churn to the battlefield. God bless Mrs. Jones. After everything she's been through—the in vitro, the Bell's palsy, the learning to make risotto—she is still somehow able to muster an appreciation for a flawless peach in the produce section, the sound of a distant woodpecker in the Dave & Buster's parking lot. When the sunset is pinker than usual, Mrs. Jones stops what she is doing and takes a picture and then she shares the picture. Not on social media, but in an *email*. In an email titled *BEAUTY IS EVERYWHERE YOU LOOK*. Mrs. Jones could have been an immigration lawyer or a judge or even a patent attorney, but she is involved in a pyramid scheme peddling collagen powder.

I know you know this, but just a refresher: Mrs. Jones has

many pairs of shoes that appear identical but aren't. The woman has an eye for subtle variation. She knows the difference between ballet flats and regular flats and skimmers and slides and mules. She's good with paint colors, too. She can help you decide between teal and peacock and pistachio and Prussian. You know what else about Mrs. Jones? She's sorry she quit piano, because the piano can bring such unexpected joy to everyday events. Like at dinner parties! How about "Camptown Races"? How about "Raspberry Beret"?

Another fun tidbit: sometimes—okay, daily—Mrs. Jones imagines having sex with people much, much younger than herself. Like, say, Kai. The Qdoba cashier. She does not imagine doing him in a somewhat respectable way, like in *The Graduate*. Not in a bed or in a hotel or surrounded by ashtrays and rolled-up pantyhose and starched white blouses draped over the backs of chairs and heavy crystal tumblers here and there bearing an inch or two of Maker's. No, she imagines ravaging Kai (and/or Kai's friends) in a frantic and furious way. Maybe in an H&M dressing room or in a damp culvert by the church soccer field. Mrs. Jones is open for business, because life is short, and you might as well go out with a bang. Or banging. Mrs. Jones's best guess is that Kai is sixteen.

Okay. Now, I see you putting your hand down. Like you never meant to wave to Mrs. Jones but instead were waving away a gnat, but you can keep on waving, because, like I said: you know her. She practically birthed you. You lived inside of her. You basically came out from between her legs and drank from her breasts.

Here comes the Joneses' son. Let's give him a name. How about Skyler? No? How about Tyler? Yes? Tyler's face says *MEH*, but his eyes say *YEAH*. He plays lacrosse but once played a cat in a school play and deep down that's all he wants to be: a gray tabby. Tyler has a secret plan. He's going to make it through high school and then get into the state college. Then, a week before college starts, Tyler is going to let his parents take him to Target to buy extra-long twin sheets and milk crates and clip-on lamps and faux-fur pillows and laundry baskets. He might let them buy him a desk blotter, even. A shower caddy. Some Pert Plus and Froot Loops. A goddamn artificial succulent or three.

After Target, Tyler is going to go through all the motions of freshman orientation. He's going to sign up for Sociology 101 and Human Development and write his name on the Ultimate Frisbee Club's clipboard. He's even going to pretend he's thinking about eventually majoring in Econ, but when school starts, Tyler won't be there. He'll be in the desert getting loaded on something that could kill an elephant. He's going to pay an internet doctor on the down-low, using the money his parents (Mr. and Mrs. Jones) thought he was going to spend on a pre-owned Mini Cooper, to have his face tattooed with stripes, his teeth filed into points. Tyler wants synthetic whiskers surgically inserted into his cheeks. He wants hair plugs all over his body like corn seedlings, row after row. A tail is not out of the realm of possibility, because it's the twenty-first century and he found a surgeon on the internet and he has cash. Anyway: Tyler has a plan and it involves a man-sized litter box, a giant jingle bell collar. But you knew that, because you know him better than you know yourself.

Of course, you remember the Joneses' daughter, Delilah. I've said it before, but I'll say it again: it's like you two were separated at birth. Delilah is beautiful but thinks she's ugly. She's smart but thinks she's stupid. She's popular but lonely, smiling but sad, thin but constantly disgusted at what she sees in the mirror. Delilah is exceptional at biology, tennis, violin, and French but the only thing she thinks she is good at is locking herself in her room and putting on her Beats by Dre and taking a Sharpie and dotting little black dots on her walls.

Delilah has to make the dots the same size and she has to space them evenly and she has to finish filling certain predetermined areas with dots before each song on her playlist ends or else she and her family will die in a horrific automobile accident or her mother will get lymphoma or she, Delilah, will start randomly hemorrhaging at school and people will think it's her period and not internal bleeding and she will never be able to show her face again, anywhere. Delilah can see it now, the blood in the hallway and the people, disgusted. The song is almost over. She'd better get those dots dotted—spaced and placed and dotted—or else she is doomed, banished and forever alone. Which you can totally understand on every level, because you basically are Delilah. Her dot game makes sense to you because you know it's not really a game. It's a prayer—*prayers*, plural— one after the other.

What else is there? I don't know if we have time today to tour the Joneses' house or go for a ride in their cars or look in their fridge or meet their dog, but I can give you a quick general overview, which will probably sound like I'm simply telling you what you already know about your own house and car and food and dog, but here I go anyway. The Joneses' house looks good from the curb, but cheap up close. There's a tinge of mildew on the aluminum siding, their doorbell sounds like a dying cow. Tyler's bunk beds are held together with a bungee cord, the master bedroom's carpeting smells faintly of broth. Delilah's bedroom is on the back of the house and she has a view of a suburban retention pond and when it doesn't rain, when there's a dry spell, the vinyl lining starts to show around the edges, reaffirming that everything in this world is fake. It's not a pond, it's a "water feature." Can you think of two sadder words together than "water" and "feature"? Neither can Delilah.

Anyway, the Joneses have a leather sectional that has not held up despite their initial enthusiasm. Two of the cushions have duct tape on them. The baseball stitching is white and synthetic and frayed like dental floss. Upstairs, downstairs, the Joneses' doorknobs are copper—plastic copper. These knobs feel lightweight and hollow in the Joneses' hands, and every time they turn a doorknob a wave of sorrow crashes over them. What is the point of this flimsy life?

But anyway, some peppier facts! The Joneses drive expensive cars—a mauve Mercedes and a bile-green Porsche Cayenne—both with high mileage and hail damage, and there's always a cold rotisserie chicken in the fridge that no one knows the age of, along with some nonalcoholic beer from that one time they tried. The Joneses' family dog? His name is Sammy. He's a rescue, a terrier mix and poorly trained, but he's the one thing they can all agree on. Look at Sammy on his back! Look at Sammy looking out the window at the squirrels! Look at Sammy! How does he do it? How does he make it look so easy and effortless? All four of the Joneses—the Mr. and the Mrs. and Tyler and Delilah—want to sit in a circle on the family room floor with Sammy in the center of the circle and they want Sammy to show them how to love. On a daily basis, the Joneses all think this and feel this in a way that brings them actual physical pain, but they cannot say it out loud to each other.

So, there you have the Joneses! Aren't they just fantastic? I knew you'd recognize them. I knew meeting them would feel redundant, like déjà vu, but still, it's always good to find your tribe, to surround yourself with people who mirror you, to be with people who *see* you, who *get* you. It makes the world seem less arbitrary, less random, like something divine and deliberate is at play. Thank God for people like the Joneses. Thank God for people like you.

Ricky

Carla felt sure she was the only rich girl to ever work the counter at Glazy's Ham Depot. Carla hadn't always been rich. Before Ed, she and her mom had once lived in a minivan for a year, so Carla remembered the ins and outs of being a have-not. Plus, her name was Carla, which was—at most—middle class. Her mother had chosen "Carla" before she'd understood the power of "Margaret" or "Paige." Because of this, Carla could hold her own at Glazy's. She parked her black Saab behind the Kmart. She left her TAG Heuer at home by the sink. Ed had gotten her the job because he owned the shopping center Glazy's was in. He said every rich kid needed one poor job on the books. Carla could write her college essay about it, Ed said.

Glazy's Ham Depot sold glazed hams. Carla's job was to "reveal" them. She and Tammy and Sonya and Richelle worked the reveals and ran the registers. In the back, guys with blurry tats and small teeth slathered corn syrup, wielded blowtorches. It was almost Christmas. There were tinsel stars taped everywhere. Carla was back in Tennessee from her Rhode Island boarding school where, to her delight, all the boys looked like surfers in houndstooth, but, to her dismay, fucked like they were hammering nails. Richelle showed Carla how to pull back the foil from a ham and sell it.

"The foil's your panties, the ham is your puss," Richelle said. Richelle never smiled. "I sell the most hams."

She pointed to the Employee of the Month pictures on the wall. There were eighteen of Richelle not smiling in her brown apron and brown hat. She had worked at Glazy's nineteen months.

"Last April, I got an abortion," she said. "It was Ricky's. I loved him. Our names went good together. He cried during sex. He bought me a pink ice ring." Richelle said "ice" like "ass." "If I'd told him about the baby, he woulda made me keep it. But where am I gonna put a baby?" Richelle looked at Carla, unblinking. "Under the goddamn counter like a goddamn ham I'm gonna steal?"

Carla's only takeaway was that she needed to meet this Ricky. She'd never heard of a guy like him. Ed talked stocks. Her missing father had talked shit. The boys at school didn't talk at all. Where was this Ricky with his emotions and simulated jewels? Did he know his way around a florist? A Hallmark? A vagina? A heart? Carla knew she should be thinking about college, a career. Shopping centers. But Richelle's story confirmed what Carla had suspected about herself all along: that she just wanted to be held, to have her hair brushed back from her face. Real estate wasn't going to look her in the eye and call out her name.

"Did Ricky work here?" Carla asked.

"Naw," Richelle said. "He worked the Valvoline." Richelle folded back a portion of gold foil to reveal a flash of pink ham.

"I'll take it," a customer said. The customer was an old woman, not even a man. Richelle had talent.

There were four Valvolines in town. Carla took her Saab to all of them. She had four different services in four days. At every one, she asked coolly: "Is Ricky working today?" She had no plan if someone said yes. If Ricky was there, what would she say? *Richelle told me about you?* She needed to keep Richelle out of it.

At the fourth Valvoline, a guy named Gunther told her Ricky now worked the Sonic on Kildeen.

"That motherfucker can roller-skate," Gunther snorted. "You believe that?"

"Wow," Carla said. "That's something."

Gunther looked at the Saab and frowned. "How you know Ricky?"

Carla stumbled in her head. "I sold him a ham."

Gunther was okay with this answer. "Oh," he said. "I like ham."

Carla went to the Sonic three times before she found Ricky. He was short, even on skates, and had a shiny, spotted face. Carla watched him weave between cars. He could spin with a tray of food. She imagined his breath in her ear. She imagined him offering her a solitary rose. She saw him with a baby. He could calm that baby down. When Ricky brought Carla the milkshake, Carla looked him right in his eyes and pulled her V-neck sweater to one side to reveal the satin cup of her bra. Ricky's eyes went big.

"Wait right here," he said.

Carla watched him skate back inside. She watched him talk to someone, take off his hat and apron, skate back to the passenger side of her car. He got into the Saab with his big skates making a fuss of the floor mat. He smelled metallic.

"I can take twenty," he said. "I know a place."

The place was a parking lot. Ricky kept his skates on. Ricky didn't cry. Ricky could hammer a nail with the best of them. Maybe Richelle was a liar. Maybe this Ricky was the wrong Ricky. One thing was certain: Carla was still poor even though she was rich, and this Ricky was rich even though he was poor. When Carla dropped Ricky back by the Sonic nineteen minutes later, Ricky skated right out of the car and back to his hat and apron. He made it look easy.

The next day at Glazy's, Carla parked her Saab right out front. She wore her TAG Heuer. On her coffee break, she called around for the morning-after pill. For the rest of the day, Carla did what she always did. She took orders. She made change. She wiped counters. She brought out ham after ham from the warming racks. She peeled back corner after corner of gold foil. She revealed glimpses of pink to the customers. Sometimes the customers nodded and paid. But more often than not, they sent the ham back for a different one. Every time, Carla went to the warming racks and brought back the same ham and pretended it was a new one. Every time, the customers nodded and paid, satisfied.

Cray

We are crazy. We are Cray. *C-R-A-Y,* Cray. We are Conrad and Ray and Apollo and Yuri. We are four boys in one. Conrad is tall and Ray is short and Apollo is night and Yuri is day, but we move and think as one. We are never alone. We are never alone when we shoplift Airheads and hair dye and condoms we have yet to use. We are never alone when we skateboard or when we are bored. We are four HEs in one WE.

We got married when Apollo and Yuri were in the sixth grade and Ray was in the fifth and Conrad was in the seventh. We met after school in the park. We met in the big stormwater drain tunnel where all of us could still stand upright, except for Conrad who is so tall he had to duck, and we gathered in a circle and took out our penises, our penii—we call the plural of "penis" "penii" with two *i*'s—and we stacked our penii the same way boys who play sports stack their hands before a game, ready to cheer. We stacked them just like that, but because most of our penii are still so small, we had to stand close together. We stood so close with our stacked penii that we could smell the stolen Airheads on each other's breath, and then we went around the circle and said, "Do you?" and each one of us had to say, "I do!" This happened four times, because there are four of us in one, and when we had all said "I do!" with authority, we brought our pants back up. We didn't kiss because that would be gay; instead, we zipped our pants in unison—*Zoop!*—and we were relieved, because we were finally married and at long last no longer alone.

On that day, we did not mention the other marriages we knew, because they were not good ones. Those marriages were between, or had been between, our mothers and our fathers, and we felt certain we were different. Those marriages were not good marriages, because those people did not love each other, and we most certainly loved each other, even though we would never say such a thing out loud. So, we were married in the tunnel and Conrad and Ray and Apollo and Yuri became Cray. And we, Cray, pulled up our pants and walked out of the tunnel into the bright May sunlight and Apollo said, "It's like being born again," and we all agreed, but we did so silently and not out loud, because Apollo has a way of saying beautiful things that make it hard to respond without your voice sounding like you are about to cry. But he was right. It was like being born again, and we came out of the tunnel feeling safe for the first time in our lives and we waded through the knee-high grass on the hill, and we went up through the ragweed and chicory and Queen Anne's lace—all that stuff that Yuri knows the name of—and a black-and-yellow butterfly landed on Ray, on one of his little ears, and we knew it was a blessing. We did not say out loud that it was a sign. Instead, we said the butterfly had landed on Ray because he was so short and so blond that the butterfly mistook him for goldenrod. And this made us laugh, long and hard. We needed the laugh after the wedding, because the wedding was such a big deal, and when our sides hurt from laughing, we simmered down into sighs and went on our honeymoon in the skate park. We set down our boards— one, two, three, four—at the top of the big ramp and we all went down together. We will all go down together.

We are Cray. We are too scared to smoke the pot that Conrad's dad smokes, because Conrad's dad has been questioned by the police twice this year and Conrad's dad talks to himself. He sees things that aren't there, like army tanks and Queen Elizabeth and bald eagles holding banners in their talons, banners that say *America is Dead* and *God is Dead*, so instead of smoking Conrad's dad's pot, we smoke Ray's mom's mullein. Ray's mom is a hippie. She makes us carob chip cookies and tells us to forgive our fathers. "The sooner you forgive your fathers, the better men you'll be," she says. We know she is right, but how do good people forgive bad people? We know we will never understand forgiveness, just like we will never understand the Dewey decimal system, but we know that, eventually, we will need forgiveness, unlike the Dewey decimal system. So, we make a silent note to try forgiving at some point for the sake of Ray's mother, because Ray's mother is beautiful—her hair is the color of October—and in the meantime, we smoke her mullein, which is some sort of a flower or weed, but not THE weed.

We steal it from her bedside table where she keeps her hot pink dildo, and this embarrasses Ray more than his height, but still, we always talk about the dildo for a while because it's a dildo, for God's sake, and when Ray looks like he might be sick, we stop talking and get back to business. We take some of the mullein for ourselves out of the wrinkled sandwich bag, and we smoke it down by the creek behind the apartment complex where Yuri lives and it makes us sleepy and it makes us talk about things we wouldn't normally talk about, like where people go when they die. Ray says when people die they just go in the ground and stop thinking and Apollo says he thinks that people go in the ground but they keep thinking forever and ever about the things they should have done and shouldn't have done. Yuri says he thinks that when we die, we all go to another dimension. That we are no longer humans or even souls, but some sort of code. That we become letters marching through some system that does something important, like an alphabet or something, being transmitted between one cosmic civilization and another. Yuri is really smart. He does good in school and he actually likes school, so when he says stuff, we believe him and this idea scares us all quiet for a good long time.

Conrad says he doesn't know where people go but he wants it to be wherever his dead dog went after the car hit him because Conrad loved that dog even more than Natalie Portman and that is saying something. Conrad once had a life-sized poster of Natalie Portman that he slept next to. And one time, when we were at his house and in his room, we saw. Near the middle of the poster was a ragged hole. A hole right where Natalie's real hole would have been. And we called him out on that. We said, "Hey, look! Conrad cut a hole in the poster. Conrad's been fucking Natalie Portman's paper hole." And we have never seen Conrad so mad. He went red and started crying the sort of crying where tears and snot and spit shoot out of a guy. The really ugly cry. "Don't talk about Natalie that way," he yelled. "Have some respect for Natalie!" He probably said that twenty or thirty times. Then he curled up in a ball on the floor of his bedroom and rocked around for a while and we just stood there and stared at him and then stared at each other and shrugged. We felt really bad, but we didn't do anything. We never do anything other than standing and waiting and shrugging when one of us is bad off. After a while, Conrad got up and rolled up the poster and put a rubber band around it, and he put it on the high shelf in his closet and wiped his face like nothing had happened. Then he said to us, "Let's go steal some Twizzlers and shit." So, we went to the old Walgreens, not the renovated one, and we stole some Twizzlers and shit. The shit was hair dye. That was the day we all dyed our hair Electric Grape at Apollo's house and ruined the downstairs sink and left before we could see the look on his mother's face.

We are Cray. We are bored. We were born bored. We will die bored. Our whole lives always have been and always will be about trying to get out of boredom. We steal our sisters' tampons and soak them in cherry Kool-Aid and sling them up to the ceiling where they dry like pink stalactites. We fart into jars and screw on the lids and dare one another to unscrew the lids and put our mouths over the jars and breathe in without breathing out. We call them "hits." *Here, take a hit.* Yuri's hits could kill a caribou. When we are tired of hits, we go to the food court and order tacos and Chinese noodles and French fries and we mix them together and eat them like it's no big thing. We steal boxes of condoms and put the condoms inside our matching duct tape wallets and walk around like we are ready for anything life throws at us.

*

We are Cray. We climb the giant pine behind the school during summer vacation and find a pile of bones in its big knothole. Yuri says they're raccoon bones, but Ray says that's no fun, and Conrad says let's pretend they're the bones of a kidnapped kid and we throw them down from the tree and climb down into the meadow and we play crime scene. We play crime scene for four hours like we aren't eleven and twelve and twelve and thirteen but six and seven and seven and eight. The sun is bright and everything seems like a dream and we are so glad we are married. When we are done with crime scene, we make a little stack of the bones and Apollo sings: *The sun is up, the sky is blue, it's beautiful, and so are you.* Goddamn Apollo. He's always trying to make us cry.

We are Cray. We don't understand girls except for our mothers. Our mothers are our churches and we go to them for comfort. We sit at their feet. They are our crosses and altars. We bring them things we find, like offerings to a god. We bring them frogs and old bananas from our lunchboxes and flowers that die the second they are picked. Our mothers are the only people we let touch us. They are the only things that give us faith. But we don't talk about our mothers that much. We steal their mullein and eat their cookies and watch them drink their Diet Cokes. We watch them fold our underwear. We worry about them, our mothers, our churches. People burn down churches, you know. We see how our mothers always smile at us, but we see how the smile wasn't there before they saw us, so we know they put the smile on their face just for us, which makes us feel special and sad. Which makes us feel like they are lying about something. Which makes us not want to grow up.

*

We are Cray. We eat nutmeg. It's Ray's idea. He says we will go on a vision quest. He brings the nutmeg and we all eat a tablespoon and then we don't feel anything, so we eat another tablespoon and then we are thirstier than we've ever been in our lives. And then Ray says he can see the end of the world in a cloud above the ballpark, like a spinning circle. Like a black hole. And then Conrad starts seeing army tanks like his dad and he curls up and cries like he did when we said he'd been fucking the Natalie Portman poster. And then Apollo starts laughing. He laughs for maybe four hours and Yuri does something with Apollo's sternum to make sure he will still get oxygen and not go brain dead. And then we go home and can't sleep, for that night or really the next, and when we meet to go skateboarding a few days later, we all just kind of sit on a bench. Something has changed. Something is changing.

We are Cry. Apollo is the first to quit showing up and without him, that's what we do: cry. We try to hide our crying by playing a game called Let's Act Like Girls and we imitate the girls in the lunchroom. We imitate their gossip. We talk about who unfriended us and who blocked us and then we say, "Ohmygod! Stop! Stop it! You're making me cry!" And then we pretend to be girls crying at a lunch table when we are just boys on a bench crying for Apollo. Our night. Our knight.

We are Cy, because Ray leaves next. Ray is the youngest and the shortest and he says he just has different things to do in his different grade and that he can't see us for a while. But we know this is a lie. We wonder what is wrong, but we cannot bring ourselves to talk about it. So, we don't steal and we don't climb and we don't skate and we don't cry. We just sigh because that's what we are now: *C-Y*, Cy. We just walk in the tall grasses that Yuri knows the names of—the fescue and thistle and timothy and yarrow—and we sigh and sigh and sigh.

We are *Y*. Because now Conrad is gone. Conrad says it is because of his dad, that he has family stuff to handle, but Yuri is the smartest and Yuri knows that it is over, and we always believe Yuri, so we all know it is over. We were Cray. We were crazy. We were crazy about each other and crazy to think it would last. But now the marriage—our marriage—is dead, like all the other marriages we know, and where do dead things go? We don't want it down in the ground, not thinking at all or forever thinking about all the things we wish we had done and wish we hadn't done. We don't want it where Conrad's dog is, because we don't know where that is. But do we want it where Yuri says the dead go? Do we want it to be broken up and broken apart? Do we want it to be parts of an alphabet? Do we want it to be letters that spell nothing? That mean nothing? Do we want to be *C* and *R* and *A* and *Y*? Do we want to go down, but not go down together?

Dawn

Cole Harding was an opener at There's a Box For That! which was indisputably the most ludicrous store in all of Pinesap Plaza. This was saying something because Pinesap was also home to Banana Pants and the Pouchy Hut and Mr. Stupid. When people needed a box—"sized cough drop to coffin!"—they went to Cole's place of employment, and he or one of his despondent coworkers found a cardboard box suited to the customer's idiotic needs. In his brief time there, eightish weeks, Cole had provided boxes for toenail clippings, guinea pig ashes, an emotional support potato, a surfboard, a Ouija board, a mounted boar's head, and a bored housewife's stallion-length autoerotic device, among other absurdities. In short, Cole had cashed out several dozen folks way sorrier than himself, which was also saying something because, just six months earlier, he had accidentally broken the neck of the homecoming queen by trying to dodge a squirrel in his mother's

Camry, and Cole didn't know what was sorrier than offing the local goddess. Well, maybe an imaginary fist fight with Henry David Thoreau. He'd been having one of those all morning, which was lamer than lame, but at least he was winning.

"Uncle!" Thoreau cried. Cole had the philosopher's arm pinned behind his back, his face pressed up against a sycamore's eye-pocked trunk. "You win! I give!"

Thoreau was wiry-strong but also, predictably, passive. He lacked an innate fury that Cole had in spades and Cole, though fleshy and washed-out and bedecked in a starched Starfleet Academy tee, was out in front thanks to his cornucopian rage.

"Is that all you got, H. D.?" Cole shouted, feigning aplomb. "Whatta you been eating? Beans?"

Up close to Thoreau's leathery nape, watching a bead of sweat travel south and magnify pores and hairs and moles, life's ugly minutiae, Cole felt the same in his make-believe world as he did in his real one: on the verge of total collapse. On the cusp of crumbling from wuss to puss. He was nothing more than a Pop-Tart eater with chalky indoor skin. A boy fresh from bluffing his way through Death Camp, a bogus retreat for mourners that had done zilch to cure him of his survivor's guilt, but where, nonetheless, he had taken home the Golden Griever award for convincing staff and fellow campers that he was okey-doke with the horseshit life could strum up. Easy-peasy with Hannah being six feet underfoot.

"Uncle!" Thoreau shouted again. "*U-N-C-L-E!*"

Cole cranked Thoreau's arm an inch higher. He could sense the fellow's rotator cuff was on the verge of something dramatic and visceral, an osteopathic grand finale, but still, Cole wasn't letting up. He would fight this fight for the same reason he'd sought out the job at There's a Box For That!—because Spectacular Trent, his Sorrow Advisor at Death Camp, had told him to. And Cole wanted to wow Trent the way Trent had wowed him.

"Have you read Thoreau?" Trent asked Cole on Day 1 of 28. "Because you should. You should read Thoreau and then do the exact opposite. Thoreau may have been hailed as the maestro of minimalism, but in reality he was nothing more than a campfire-building candy-ass."

Cole knew Thoreau. Everything the man had done or stood for sounded sublime. A crude shelter? A hard cot? *Self-reliance*? To live in a place where hunger outweighed heartache sounded beyond idyllic. Maybe if Cole pulled a full-on Henry David, he could quit thinking of the car crash and start thinking of immediate things: the wind chill, his thirst, a blister, the croup. Maybe the thunder of a melting spring pond could drown out the image of Hannah, passenger seat, eyes wide, soul gone, his fault. Too bad, then, that Spectacular Trent was so spectacular. He had a way of doing something to—or undoing something inside of—everybody.

"Don't buy into the New Age goulash served up here, Cole Slaw. All the other Sorrow Advisors are filling campers' bowls with charlatan chili and the campers are lapping it up. Grief and guilt make you a hungry, hungry hippo. But stay strong. Don't be a pantywaist," Trent reiterated on Day 2 of 28. "Any old pansy can hide and deny. The only way to peace, Cole, is through chaos." Spectacular Trent cracked his wide bronze neck and flared his nostrils in a decisive way. "Seek out the most maddening place you can think of. Then put your ass smack dab in the center of it and let the pain pass through you like a sword. Pain kills pain, Cole. Invite torture into your heart."

Spectacular Trent gave his mane a toss and stood Christlike in the middle of the archery field. Trent was so fully Trent that Cole wanted to please him the same way he'd wanted to please Hannah, who'd been so fully Hannah. Right then and there, on Day 2.5, Cole decided to do and say the things a boy might do and say to make an idol think he was someone other than who he was. Cole began fast putting forth the illusion that he was fully capable of overcoming the insurmountable. That Hannah's death was a hill he could trot over in old sneakers, given a lazy afternoon and some granola bars.

"Uncle!" Thoreau shouted a final time. "Uncle Tom's Cabin!"

Cole, at last gripped with some sort of existential mercy, released Thoreau's arm. He opened and closed the drawer to the cash register. He wiped the counter with a wet wipe. He assumed the pronounced slump he reserved for first shifts. And then he stared, glazed, out into the mall. The first batch of Pouchies at the Pouchy Hut was being deep fried. Over at Shake Your Booty, the Doc Martens Cole had his eye on were still on display, soles soft, tongues wagging. In the Grand Atrium, the month's shopping theme was being assembled. This one, "Great Americans," thus far featured a half-inflated Muhammad Ali and an Abraham Lincoln scarecrow still face down on the Astroturf. Another laughable day at Pinesap Plaza was dawning. Just as the sun had risen over Walden, the singing fluorescents were starting their morning flutter above the mall's roaring sterile fountain. Before long, someone wide and desperate would waddle to its concrete shores, toss in a penny and sigh. Cole had done as Trent had commanded. He had planted his ass smack dab in the center of madness. But the pain was not passing though Cole like a sword. Instead, it was trapped within him, a short dagger twisting.

*

Halfway between agony and lunch, the girl appeared in the doorway of There's a Box For That! like some sort of savior. She wore a hospital gown tucked madly into oversized cargo shorts, as well as a pair of disposable flip-flops, the sort Cole had seen scuffing out of Nail Perfecto at the dark end of the mall. The girl's hair was the loud, artificial color of something tropical. Mangoes, maybe. Guava? Papaya? Whichever, whatever, Cole felt something expand in him when she appeared—relief, wonder, testosterone—he couldn't say.

"Here's the question of the day." The girl came up to the counter, breathless and darty-eyed. "What's your smallest of small?"

The question felt personal and Cole shifted in his pants. Then he looked and saw: in the crook of the girl's left arm was worn white tape, on her wrist a blue plastic hospital bracelet, of which Cole could read half. *AURORA FLOO* . . . What sort of last name started that way? Floozy? Aurora reached down into her shorts' pocket, then she brought out her fist, which she thrust toward Cole like she wanted him to guess what was inside.

"How small can a box be?" she said. "Because this here's as small as it gets." Aurora turned over her fist and opened her palm to reveal a black speck that Cole assumed to be a gnat, dead.

"A dead bug?" he said. "A box for that?"

Aurora shook her head aggressively. "It's a seed," she said. "And nobody so far has believed me when I tell them what it grows. They were all: 'Oh sure, Aurora. That's a real nice seed you've got there. Real nice, sweetheart. And I'm sure it grows what you say it grows, but why don't you come with me for a minute after you finish your broth?' And then the next thing I know I'm going from the floor with the braindeads to the floor with the nutjobs."

Cole looked down but the girl's fist had closed back up around the speck good and tight. The store was empty save for her. Earlier there'd been a man looking for a box to hold a knife made from a deer antler. "Make a weapon out of the thing you've killed to kill another one of those things," he'd said. Then a woman had come in with seven bras the color of pancake batter. "I want a box for each one. One for every day of the week." After the bra woman, there'd been no one for a long time. Cole had grown bored, then sullen, then panicked. He'd gone down to the Pouchy Hut and eaten two Pouchies. A Frooty Tooty and a Hoomungus Fungus. He'd sat by the deafening fountain and crammed the strawberry pie and the mushroom pie into his mouth. Both had made him nauseous and sad. Eating Pouchies always brought him to the verge of vomit and tears. But now, here was Aurora with her mai tai hair and trembling voice and the more Cole looked at her the better he felt. She put forth the sort of desperation Cole had packaged and frozen within himself, a roast wound and compressed in plastic wrap.

"I was in a coma for thirteen days after the fall. Fourteen is when they really start to freak out on you, but I woke up right before that because I've always been just decent enough to my parents." Aurora looked at Cole straight on. "You know where the comatose go? Because I'll tell anyone who'll listen and you seem like a listener. Are you a listener? Don't answer me, just hear me out. The comatose live between this world and the next. You probably won't believe that, nobody does, but we go to the moon. To its dark side. Over there, there's a stadium. We call it the ComaDome. It's big and white and we're all just sitting there inside it in our hospital gowns, waiting. Sometimes the person next to you disappears. Did they die? Did they go back? These are the things you wonder."

Now Cole wasn't thinking about boxes. He wasn't thinking about Hannah. He wasn't thinking about Thoreau or the dough in his stomach or the batter-colored bras or the deer knife. He wasn't thinking about how he'd picked up Hannah in the rain. How he'd convinced her to let him give her a ride to volleyball. He wasn't thinking about how she'd slumped down in the passenger seat so as not to be seen with him. He wasn't thinking about what happened next. And he certainly wasn't thinking about the visitation. About all the wailing and the glossy pink coffin covered in purple carnations and how Hannah's boyfriend, Dirk, had punched his fist through an oil painting of a Victorian woman holding two babies with bluebirds on their crotches. He wasn't thinking about all the people who hated him, who wished him dead. He wasn't thinking about pulling the dagger out of his insides and running it down his wrists. He wasn't thinking about how his father no longer spoke. How his mother cried when she looked at his face. Cole wasn't thinking about anything. All he was doing was watching Aurora talk. Her words were like a song he had heard a long time ago. A lullaby.

"Once a girl who was sitting beside me in the ComaDome just up and vanished. Then two minutes later she was back. 'I died,' she said. 'I went to the next place,' she said. 'Heaven?' I said. 'No,' she said. 'The Garden.' 'Of Eden?' I said. 'No,' she said. 'The Olive Garden.' 'The restaurant?' I said. 'No,' she said. 'The Garden of Olives.' Then she held out her hand for me to see and in her hand were two seeds."

Aurora held out her fist again to demonstrate, but she did

not open it this time. Now Cole could read her last name on the bracelet: FLOOD.

"'These seeds grow the trees in the next place,' the girl said. And I said, 'Those don't look like olive seeds. Those aren't pits.' And she said, 'Not all the trees in the Olive Garden are olive trees, you idiot.' And then she gave me one seed and kept the other for herself and we both sat there in our hospital gowns staring straight ahead with the seeds in our hands and after a while she said, 'I can hear my mother begging. I can hear my father crying. Goddamn it. How selfish can they be? I cannot bring myself to go back to that place.' And I wondered: which place is she talking about? The next place—the Olive Garden? Or Earth? Is she talking about home? And then she turned to me and said, 'If you're unlucky enough to go back to the first place, you need to plant that seed I gave you. Plant it in the most terrible place you can find so that place stands half a chance.' And then she disappeared for a final time and I knew she was at the Olive Garden and I knew I was going back to the hospital before long with this seed. And that's why I'm here. The seed needs a box. I mean, I'm going to plant it, but until I find the most terrible place to plant it, I need a place to put it."

Cole stared at Aurora's mouth a final time. He wanted to press his own against it. Not so much for a kiss, but so the story inside of Aurora could pass from her to him. So, the story could go down inside him and pull out the dagger. Cole thought about this, the story and dagger battling it out, like he and Thoreau had, and Aurora just looked at him and frowned. She held out her fist again and then pounded a little pound on the countertop. "You got a box or not?" she said. "That's why I'm here!"

Cole gave a jerk and apologized. He motioned down an aisle

and nodded and Aurora proceeded down the aisle and Cole followed behind. As the girl walked, her cargo shorts slipped a bit, and when she yanked them up, something dropped to the cold tile. Cole thought it was another seed, but when he bent over, he saw it was a pill. Bright blue, the color of a happy sky, and about the size of a small beetle. Aurora didn't notice, so Cole plucked it up from the ground the same way Thoreau might a berry. He'd save it for a time when he could really use it. He hoped it might do something to him that had never been done before.

Hannah hadn't had the luxury of going comatose. Her neck had snapped right after Cole had done his little zigzag game with the squirrel, right after the zigzag led to the elm. Cole and his zigging and zagging had sent the volleyball captain straight to the Olive Garden. He'd done the zigzag because that was all Cole had to offer someone like Hannah. That and math. Hannah had been assigned to work with Cole on a chemistry project. Hannah had made the gagging sign with her finger when Cole's name had been called by the teacher. Cole hadn't cared. He'd done all the work, all the research, all the writing. All Hannah had had to do was hold a poster that Cole had made and roll her beautiful eyes while Cole told the class everything there was to know about the project.

"I'm presenting the project," he said. "Because Hannah did everything else."

He'd been willing to lie for her. To die for her. She was divinity, he was disciple. There was no god beyond earth, Cole felt sure. But there were gods on earth. Hannah, Spectacular Trent. Cole had killed one trying to impress her. He'd kill himself trying to impress the other.

"It was a deer," Cole had told the cops. "Two," he'd said. "A doe and a fawn." This had been at the hospital. Cole had sprained his pinkie. Hannah's parents were in another room, on top of Hannah's lifeless body, flopping, heaving, like walruses. Cole had a little splint on his hand with bubblegum pink foam to cushion his finger. "The fawn still had spots," Cole said. He'd heard somewhere that spots meant a deer was a newborn. "I swerved so I wouldn't kill it. Then I swerved again to miss its mother. Then I hit the tree."

The story played well to the police. Better than the zigzag would have. Better than him driving with his knees and him playing Pink Floyd and him not wearing his horn-rims and him all "Watch this!" would have. But Dirk & Company weren't the police. Dirk & Company let everyone know they would have chosen to hit the deer, to be on a different road, to go slower, to drive better, to own a safer, more expensive car.

"Who swerves?" Dirk had asked.

"Who swerves?" everyone repeated.

WHO SWERVES? posters were hung at school. *WHO SWERVES?* was carved into Cole's locker with a key. His mother eventually pulled him from school to homeschool him, but all she did was let him sleep, watch *Star Trek*. His father had started drinking. His father knew nothing about alcohol. He was a short, shy computer programmer who stuttered. But he went out and bought rum. He drank the rum in a coffee cup and quit talking. His mother's lip always quivered when she smiled. At night, when he tried to sleep, Cole kept seeing the squirrel. Every time he saw it, he ran right over it. *Pip, pop.* Life went on as intended.

At the visitation, Cole held out his pink-splinted pinkie and shook Hannah's parents' limp hands. Hannah's father looked gray. Hannah's mother had white clumps in the corners of her mouth. Hannah's sister told him to go fuck himself. "With a fucking chainsaw." Cole's parents led him to a corner of the funeral home and gave him a small Styrofoam plate with three baby carrots and a circle of ranch on it. Cole ate them robotically and then regurgitated them into a peace lily.

When he went to Death Camp, Cole read *Walden* again when Trent wasn't looking. Cole knew then who wouldn't have swerved: Thoreau. Thoreau wouldn't have zigzagged. Thoreau would have stopped the car. Good ol' Henry David would have put on his hazards and gotten out of the car and called to the doe, the fawn, the squirrel. The animals would have come to him. And when the animals came to him, Hannah would have come to him. She would have watched how the animals ate straight from his palm. When they were finished, she would have taken his palm and kissed it, pressed it to her heart. Hannah would have fallen in love.

Cole put the blue pill into the tiniest box the store sold, the cough drop one, when Aurora wasn't looking. Then he held out an identical box, and Aurora dropped in the seed. When Aurora bent down to remove her puka shell anklet—"It's the only money I have"—Cole switched the boxes once, then twice, then six times, swirling them on the counter like a magician, until he didn't know which one held the seed and which one held the pill. He chose one and put it in his pocket.

"I might plant it right here in the mall someday," Aurora said, straightening. She slid her anklet toward Cole and he slid it back, shrugging. "This place is terrible all right."

Cole didn't want to stop hearing the things Aurora had to

say. He wanted to look at her cantaloupe hair and her chapped wide mouth and scared round eyes for as long as she would let him. Would he see her again? "Maybe at the real Olive Garden," he said. "I mean the restaurant one."

"What?" Aurora said. Now she had the box, the remaining one, in her fist. Her hand could almost cover it. It was a very small box. Cole had done a good job. He had done one thing right.

"The seed," Cole said. "You could plant it at the restaurant."

"Oh," Aurora said. She rolled her eyes like Hannah had holding the poster. "Right."

Cole wanted to say *You know where to find me*, but instead he said, "You should go now."

So, Aurora went. She shuffled back out into the mall in her disposable flip-flops and sagging shorts. Watching her go, Cole felt like he was at another funeral. This one was also his fault. He could smell another batch of Pouchies frying up. Even though his shift wasn't over, he went out into the mall. He went down to the Grand Atrium and saw that Muhammad Ali was now fully inflated. Abraham Lincoln was still face down, but next to him, the display crew had set up a small pop-up tent. It was painted to look like a cabin, thick stripes of brown, thin stripes of white. Cole walked right into the display, right over Lincoln, and got down on his knees. No one noticed. No one cared. Cole darted his eyes like Aurora, just to be sure, then he crawled right inside the little cabin and lay with his legs poking out the front.

Inside the cabin, Cole closed his eyes and listened to the roar of the fountain, the periodic squeak of sneaker. He smelled the new batch of Pouchies and guessed they were Little Piggies. He tried to think of God. He saw the mall Santa Claus in his elastic beard. He saw Spectacular Trent and Hannah. Maybe it would have been better if Hannah had gone to the ComaDome. If her parents had been given more time to say goodbye. Cole wondered what Trent did the rest of the year. He remembered one camper had said he was a bartender. That from September to May, Spectacular Trent was Shitfaced Trent. *Don't tell me that.* Cole had begged. *Leave me with something.*

A tear rolled out of each shut eye. Cole let the tears roll into his ears. He thought of boxes. He saw Hannah in one of the surfboard boxes with seven bras and a deer knife. He saw the box get soggy, the worms get in.

"Don't think like that," a voice said. "Don't beat yourself up like you did me." Cole opened his eyes and saw Thoreau, his head at least, poking into the cabin. "Come with me," Thoreau said. "I'll show you which way she went."

Cole sat up as best he could in the little fabric cabin. He squeezed through the front flap and out into the maddening Grand Atrium. The people were as dense as a forest. They stared with big birch eyes. They talked, all of them all at once, like a murder of crows. Cole pushed through them, past forest, past eyes. When he was on the verge of giving up, he saw her, a flash of her hair on the horizon. A slice of watermelon pink like the first glimpse of dawn. Cole quickened his pace. He threw limbs against limbs. He brought the tiny box from his pocket and shook it high above his head. Thoreau was nowhere to be found.

"Aurora!" Cole called. "It's me!"

Aurora turned and looked. She didn't see Cole, but he saw her. She was still within reach. If Cole could get to her before she disappeared, it would be the start of a new day.

Nine Dreams about Marriage

On the first dream, there's a bull shark in a dim, underground bar. The bar smells of keg beer and cigarettes. It's not before the smoking ban, it's just one of those bars where people smoke like there never was a smoking ban. The same song keeps playing from the jukebox, but no one can see where the jukebox is. Only the bull shark seems to know its location. He's put in five dollars of quarters and Led Zeppelin's "The Ocean" on repeat.

The bull shark sits at the bar on a cherry leather barstool like he owns the place, which he might. His name is Boss. He's a seven-footer, three hundred pounds and painfully handsome—almost electric blue in the dim light. He has a few dozen dark scars on his sharkskin, not from noble fights or run-ins with boats but from secret self-mutilation. Down inside, Boss suffers from insecurity, abysmal loneliness, but he calls his pain boredom. He will always call his pain boredom, because awareness and self-love are lost causes for bull sharks.

"Beefeater," he says to the bartender, and the bartender pours him four ounces of gin and the bull shark tosses the gin over his gills, a splash over his left shoulder, the rest over his right. By the end of the night, Boss is surrounded by remoras, all of them resisting what they do best—clinging, hanging on for dear life—and all of them hoping to suck him. Remoras are, no surprise, Anxious Attachment types, which is equally repellent and intriguing to Boss, who, like all sharks except for the whale shark, is Avoidant Attachment.

At last call, Boss nods at the smallest remora, who gasps in gratitude and gets to work, right there, under the bar, no shame in her game.

The next part of the dream is where Boss and the remora get married. After the wedding ceremony, they turn into humans: your parents. Your mother, the remora, spends her whole life sucking and cleaning. Sometimes she breaks down and screams at your father, the Boss, and says: "All I am to you is a whore and a maid! A goddamned hooker and a goddamned housekeeper!" Your father finds her anger amusing, but he knows better than to smile. "Now, now," he says. "You're also a nurse."

Inevitably, your mother sticks around for the free ride. How would she get anywhere without your father? He's big and fast. No one dares bother your mother when she's with him.

When your mother was a little girl, she would sit at her bedroom window and gaze out at the neighbors' blue Mercedes and wait for the tiny wife in tiny heels to come out of the house like a bright idea. She would wait for the wife to go to the car and open its big door and get inside and drive away. When your mother was a little girl, this was the only wish she ever thought to make.

The second dream goes something like this: there's this girl in a parking lot on a hot summer day. She's removing the gold from her neck and wrists, the piercings from her lobes and lips. She's lifting up her shirt and taking jewelry out of her nipples and navel. You see her peeling off her artificial nails. Taking out her false teeth. She's putting all these clattering, chattering things into a little woven basket like she's about to go through airport security, except where she's going is church. She's in a church parking lot. You're realizing that now. And also that the basket is actually an offering basket.

Except the girl doesn't go into the church. She goes to the back of the parking lot and climbs into the dumpster. It's like you're there with her, in the dumpster, because you can see, in Technicolor, what it is the devout actually discard: candle stubs, disposable coffee cups, chocolate doughnuts with one bite taken out of them. There's even a teen's secret baby. It's fresh and wet, lilac and silent. It might belong to the girl, you can't say for sure. But there she goes, sitting down in the dumpster and dumping out the offering basket. You can hear her adornments, her acrylic tips and diamond studs, rattling down through the trash, sure and steady, like sleet through a pine tree. The girl goes: "I'm sorry. I'm so sorry." Is she saying it to you or to herself or to God or to the baby?

When the girl is done apologizing, she climbs out of the dumpster and walks to her house. You sit on the curb, in the hot sun, and wait for her. Eventually, she reappears in an eyelet sundress and silk, chartreuse, ballet flats. She carries a dainty chartreuse handbag full of popcorn. She starts walking to the courthouse and you follow her. She never notices you're there, but somehow you know that you're on your way to get married. On the courthouse steps, the pigeons form a ring around you and the girl. The birds wear neckties of amethyst and emerald and sapphire and gasoline. Both of you just stand there and listen to them coo. It's the sound of blood in a vein.

The third dream is one of those fast, falling dreams. In it, you think of a widow, named Joy, who no longer knows herself. And then you wake up startled, unsure of what day it is.

The fourth dream takes place at a law firm, in the breakroom, by the copy machine. There's a guy, Forrest, and a girl, Fern. To them their names seem like destiny even though neither says so out loud. Fern imagines thriving at Forrest's feet and Forrest imagines sheltering Fern from harm. Both Forrest and Fern are rising sophomores at elite colleges that have been used as film locations for slasher movies. Both are unpaid summer interns toting accordion files bursting with divorce papers. His divorce involves a tycoon, a tramp, and a teetotaler. Hers is less alliterative. "Just a dick and a bitch," she says. You almost wake up laughing, but then you realize it's a dream and you make it keep going.

Forrest and Fern discover the breakroom door can be locked. Fern leans over the copy machine and lifts her blouse. The lace of her bra comes out nicely, a silhouette of winter frost; her beauty mark is a dot of ink—her hopes, punctuated. Forrest goes next. He unzips his pants and leans over the copy machine as if urinating into a well. He smiles. His face lights up once by a flash of lightning.

Fern refuses to look at Forrest's copy. She makes him turn it over when he hands it to her. Then they both take the paper copies and fold them into tight squares the size of crackers. They bring the crackers together. *Cheers.*

"I'm never getting married," the girl says.

"I'm never getting divorced," the boy says.

They are both wrong. Fern will get married and Forrest will get divorced. You know this is what will happen, because you're the one having the dream. You're the one who gets to decide.

The fifth dream occurs in November, on a farm. Out in the bleak cornfields, there's a farmhand snaring rabbits with picture wire and turnip tops. He brings home two limp bodies to his wife. They are eastern cottontails the color of bread crusts. You can't touch them in the dream, but you know they are as warm as a pair of gloves just removed.

The farmhand's wife makes stew from the meat.

The farmhand makes earmuffs from the pelts.

When the farmhand eats the stew, he is filled with desire.

When the wife puts on the earmuffs, the only thing she can hear is her own racing heart.

You always wake up from this dream crying.

Is the wife's heart racing because she's in love, or is it racing because she's prey?

In this dream, the sixth one, your name is Bernard and God is your husband.

Every morning, you bring him rye toast on a pink plate. You bring it to him in bed and say, "I made you breakfast, God." And he says, "Well, I made you, Bernie."

And then he eats without getting crumbs in the sheets, because God is good in bed.

In dream seven, you're in a horse stall with Mason Delaney. The stall is full of fresh straw and lime, and the sun is shining through the bars of the stall, striping Mason's body, making him into the tiger he is. You and Mason have a plan to elope in his Datsun with a box of white cupcakes and a Mastercard. Every time in this dream, your father finds the two of you in the stall. And, every time in this dream, your father punches Mason with a punch so hard that Mason's teeth go scattering on the packed dirt of the barn floor like a strand of pearls ripped from a throat.

That's where the dream always ends: you on your knees, naked, gathering the teeth, trying to say *STOP! STOP!* but unable to speak.

Dream eight. You're at this party where you don't know anyone, but this woman named Candy introduces herself to you at the dessert table. You're grateful to have someone to talk to, but Candy starts telling you everything about herself and her life before you can even help yourself to some cake, and the cake looks really good. You don't normally eat cake, but in this dream the cake is just phenomenal looking. Eight layers high. Deep maroon. Dusted with powdered sugar that is somehow lavender. How is it lavender?

Candy explains that she has spent her whole life taking care of others. From age five to age eight, there was her mother, the colostomy bag, the broth tipped from a spoon, the morphine dropped under her mother's tongue, her mother's arms reaching toward the ceiling like a child asking to be picked up.

"HOSPICE!" Candy explains, loudly, even though the party is not loud. "THAT'S WHERE YOU GET THE MORPHINE DROPS!"

Then from age eight to age twelve, there was Candy's father. The back pills and the rage, the cliff he'd walked off of, his bones found by hikers nine months later. Bones that Candy and her uncle had to buy a child's casket for.

"CHEAPER!" Candy shouts. "BUT SADDER!"

Then from age twelve to age twenty, there were Candy's siblings: Ambler, Best, and Eustice. They'd needed their macaroni mixed with powdered cheese and their hair combed free of nits and help writing their letters and constant reassurance that Candy wasn't going to die from a bad stomach or walk off a cliff from a bad mind.

This whole time Candy's talking, you're looking at the cake and wondering if it's going stale. Getting dry. It still looks moist. Will you ever get to it? How many more people has Candy cared for? Get on with it, Candy.

Candy starts in next on the animals. The stray cats and the litter of raccoons that she fed with her milky fingertips and the two dogs with three legs, and then she's back on people: Zaine, the neighbors' boy that the neighbors didn't want, and then all the babies at the daycare and then, of course, J.C. J.C. had jumpstarted Candy's car at the county fair and she'd thanked him for taking care of her, but before he could get the cables back into his truck, they'd locked eyes, and Candy knew that look, because it was the only look she knew.

"IT'S THE ONLY LOOK I KNOW!" Candy shouts in the dream. "A DOG KICKED! A WOMAN SCORNED! A CHILD ABANDONED! A MAN LOST! THAT'S MY

LOOK, SISTER! IT'S GOT MY NAME ALL OVER IT!"

You think the cake that you can't reach in the dream is red velvet cake. But it's dark enough to maybe be devil's food, while also still red enough to maybe be cherry. Black cherry? Cherry cola? That powdered sugar though. It's purple, right? A pale purple? Or is it just the lighting?

Candy goes on to tell you that she took in J.C. that very night. The night of the jumper cables. She made him a plate of biscuits and a place on the sofa with a clean sheet tucked around the cushions, because that's who she was. That's what she did. People always thought she and God must be real tight, but Candy didn't much believe in him. She supposed she believed in doing all the things God wanted people to do, but him as a person, he just wasn't her type. Candy didn't need a church to tell her what she should and shouldn't be doing. Her conscience was for that. Plus, on Sundays, she had to feed everyone: Ambler, Best, and Eustice, and all their kids. Candy couldn't waste the day sitting in a pew listening to things she already knew when she could be home making chili and cornbread and marshmallow Jell-O salad and jugs of instant tea set out in the sun with sugar like snowdrifts in the bottom. Church wasn't going to make Candy any better. Her only sin was the eating and she wasn't going to stop eating.

"I HAVE TO BE BIG!" she shouts. "I HAVE TO BE EVERYTHING TO EVERYONE! AT ANY ONE TIME THERE ARE FIVE SOMEBODIES HANGING OFF ME! I CAN'T AFFORD TO LET THEM DOWN BY BEING A RAIL OF A THING!"

After this, Candy eats the cake. All of it except for one bite. You watch her eat it, and then, while she's still chewing the last of it, except for that one bite, J.C. shows up to pick her up. He comes into the party like some sort of groupie, and he looks at Candy the same way you've been looking at the cake all night.

"I MARRIED HIM!" Candy says before she walks out the door, pointing at J.C. "SPOILER ALERT!"

When Candy is gone, you eat that last bite. It tastes like nothing you've ever had and nothing you ever will have again.

Dream nine. You and Corey meet for the first time on the ferry. You have the smokes and Corey has the vodka disguised in a Sprite can. Neither of you have a lighter, which you both refer to as "flame."

"Got any flame?" you both say.

"Jinx," you both say.

"Buy me a Coke," you both say.

You go around the deck looking for someone with fire. It's windy and the wind whips your long hair into salty ropes. You have to yell a little, even though you don't know each other from Adam. This shouting makes you instant family, like you're going back and forth in some kitchen at Thanksgiving, getting hot. While you look for fire, you share cavalier sips from the Sprite can like you've swapped spit in other ways. Eventually, you find a guy your age wearing a collegiate baseball cap backward.

"Hey, Biff," Corey says. "Got a light?"

The wind takes Corey's words right into your ear like an inside joke. You feel yourself go damp between the legs and warm in the face. The guy pulls a silver Zippo from his flannel shirt's chest pocket. He zigzags the lighter on his denim hip until a flame appears, then he cups his hand and goes to light your Marlboros as if he's just swung down from a mustang.

"Easy now, Lone Ranger," Corey says, taking the lighter

from him. "We can handle the physics of firing up our own Reds."

The guy's face flickers with disbelief then falls in disgust. "Dykes," he mutters.

You and Corey snort like he's crazy, but it's clear in the split second your eyes lock over the Zippo that maybe the guy is onto something true and terrifying.

"Here's your fancy Bic back," Corey says after she lights her cigarette and exhales in his direction. "We lesbians appreciate your chivalry."

The guy has heard enough. He huffs away, turning his cap around as he does so, and you and Corey stand victorious at the bow of the boat, smoking in tandem. It's then that you can see the island in the distance for the first time, a dirty thought gaining traction in the June haze.

"Just one dig," Corey says flatly, "and he went from Superman to serial killer."

She takes a deliberate, final drag, flicks her butt out into the Atlantic. You do the same to keep the dance alive, before taking a long sideways look at Corey. The early summer mist is all over her—her knotted hair, her eyelashes, the faintest fur along her jawline. It's all dew and cobwebs, and for a moment you feel like you might burst into tears. You crack your knuckles on your temple. The ferry chugs eastward. The dark dream of an island appears for good now.

"Guys wear hats to let you know they're schooled, when school is nothing more than a load of horseshit," Corey says. "What do you remember from school this year? Because here's what I remember: Mira Kinnison shitting herself during the school play but not the quadratic formula."

"I took German," you say. "For what?"

"Her shit was the color of stone-ground mustard, but don't ask me to graph an X and a Y." Corey finishes the vodka. "You know what I'll remember when I'm eighty? Mira Kinnison. But the Treaty of Ghent? Stab me." Corey pauses, closes her eyes like she's in throes of existential pain, then sneezes.

"Gesundheit," you say. "That's German."

"My name's Corey," Corey says.

"My name's Trapp," you say.

"My summer job on the island is at a bed-and-breakfast." Corey says. "Washing sheets."

"I don't have a job," you say. "At least not yet."

You see the dewdrops are gone from Corey's lashes, but the lashes are still wet, stuck together in dark triangles like a doll's. "Work with me," Corey says.

You say nothing. Which you suppose is a way of saying yes. And then, there it is, the island. No longer a dirty thought, but a decent one. Emerald green and dotted with white and red and blue. The sun is high and bright. The mist is gone. The sea birds rain down like black and white confetti. A hush settles over you and Corey like a fever or fear. You are out of your element altogether, but you are together. And when the ferry pulls in and blows its loud horn, even it is unable to break the spell between the two of you.

This is one of those dreams that never seems to end. The kind that goes on all night—like for nine hours, uninterrupted. In the next part, you're at the bed-and-breakfast. The one Corey mentioned on the ferry. It's called The Cliffs after the couple who owns it, Cliff Hampstead and Cliff Quincy, who was originally Owen Quincy before he'd fallen in love with Cliff Hampstead at a wedding.

"It was a wedding for a fellow named Ezra and a girl named Maryland—like the state—and Ham and I were sitting at a far table sharing a secret joint when we both said, like we were two fucking fortune tellers, THIS WON'T LAST!"

"I hadn't smoked weed in fifteen years," Hampstead says.

"And I hadn't been in love in fifteen days," Quincy adds.

"But when we both said the same thing at the same time," Hampstead says.

"We were jinxed. We just locked eyes and passed the joint under the tablecloth and six weeks later we were out here," Quincy says.

"On a fucking cliff," Hampstead says.

"Some pot that was," Quincy finishes.

The two men look at one another like dogs do owners. They're dressed in sky-blue pants and sorbet-colored sweaters and sipping drinks through striped paper straws. Cliff Hampstead has a large, handsome head as square as a birdhouse. Cliff Quincy is frail and thin. You can't look at him without hearing the snap of wood. You notice Hampstead can't look at him without getting teary. Time is of the essence in some way that you have yet to decipher.

"Every day at ten, you ladies will go to the guesthouse and get the linens," Hampstead says, pointing at an outbuilding with good posture. "And then you'll take them back to The Engine," he says, pointing at one that slouches.

"The Engine is just a ridiculous name for the garage," Quincy says. "It's where the washer is. Along with Hammy's tinker toy."

Hampstead shrugs. "So, sue me. I have a Porsche."

"A pink one." Quincy groans. "And it's been on blocks for

six years. On blocks! A Porsche! What a sin. The original one, if you ask me."

You look at Corey in the hopes she will look at you, but Corey is staring out at the sea in a serious way that reminds you that you know nothing whatsoever about her.

"Just ignore the car," Hampstead says. "All you have to worry with are the linens."

"And they're worry enough," Quincy says. "You have to strip them, spot treat them, wash them, dry them, iron them."

"Then fold them, in the case of towels," Hammy says.

"And make the beds in the case of sheets," Quincy adds.

"It's not hard work. Just time-consuming. And it's time-consuming because it has to be done every day."

"'Has to be' is a matter of debate," Quincy says. "We just believe it should be."

There is a pause in the wind, during which Hammy sighs, loudly and suddenly serious. "All good things take time, and then the next thing you know there's no more time at all."

You and Corey and the two Cliffs stand outside the tall shingled farmhouse on a square of green lawn. Quincy considers a gull fighting the breeze; Hampstead considers Quincy; Corey continues staring down the far, gray Atlantic—not the blue stretch you came in on, but the deviant one beyond. You, now convinced you've made a mistake or three, distract yourself with a visual tour of the property. There is the proper guesthouse on its own patch of fescue; there is The Engine, slouching on a circle of gravel, where you and Corey will stay; there is the long, unruly grass, like parched summer hair, waving this way and that between the buildings. You turn back to the green lawn underfoot, then point to where, past the house, a stretch of turf has been plowed up into a black crumble of soil. "What goes there?" you ask to everyone's audible relief.

Hampstead and Quincy burst into laughter.

"You tell her," Hampstead says.

"We're pregnant," Quincy says.

"Come and see!" they sing as one.

The four of you go out to the black crumble to meet the baby. It's a pumpkin, the size of a volleyball and the color of free-range egg yolk. It's nestled under a firm and decisive leaf, a parent's hand held out in salute. "It's an Atlantic Giant," Hampstead says. "Starting next week, she's slated to put on ten pounds a day."

"By Labor Day, four hundred pounds a week." Quincy says.

"And by Halloween, our daughter should be one ton of fun."

"We blanket her at night," Quincy says, "with my Aunt Diana's silk quilt." Quincy points to the clothesline he had pointed to earlier, when you and Corey had asked about a clothes dryer. *It blows something fierce up here, darlings.* "We'll keep her warm till the end."

Corey, finally back from assessing the sea, crosses her arms and shakes her head. "And then what?" she asks. "What comes after that?"

Hampstead and Quincy go silent. You wonder why on earth Corey would say such a thing. In your mind, an orange balloon loses all of its air until it's nothing more than a soft sliver of rotten rind. There's a possibility Corey has a real mean streak, and now, here you are, poised to share a futon with her for ninety days.

"Death," Quincy says simply. "That's what comes next."

You watch Hampstead watch Quincy. The wind picks up on cue, so determined and self-confident, spiteful even, that you feel certain it will take all ninety pounds of Quincy up and away.

"That's Quincy for you," Hampstead says quietly. "Always giving away the ending."

The dream goes on.

In the garage, the convertible Porsche is displayed top down, exposed and captive, like a pink woman at the mercy of someone else. When the Cliffs go back to the farmhouse, and their yellow upstairs window turns black, Corey climbs right inside of the car and closes its door with an expensive thump. She sits behind the wheel and runs her hands all over the leather seats in a territorial fashion. You stand by the washing machine, inwardly appalled, with an unaffected look on your face. Outside the wind has died down. It's finally getting dark, though it's nearly ten. *Where are we?* you wonder. *The North Pole? Santa's workshop?* You've never been this close to the top of the map in the summertime. Will the sun rise before deep sleep? Above, a ceiling fan goes around, slow and lopsided, accomplishing nothing. Corey produces an unlit cigarette and puts it between her lips. She looks at you, once again in need of a flame. You rummage around The Engine's shelves and cabinets until you find a soft book of matches. You go to the driver's side where Corey sits waiting, and you light a match and hold it out to Corey who leans forward, puffing her cheeks like a pro and squinting her eyes.

"My parents' first date was in a convertible," Corey says, smoking and talking with both hands on the steering wheel. "Climb in and we'll go nowhere just like they have."

You resist. You hold the burnt match to your nose and think of birthdays, fireworks, causes for celebration.

"My mother got shit-housed last fall and told me she slept with my father on their first date. 'That's a mistake, Corinne. The sooner you give it up, the sooner they give up on you.'" Corey makes her voice ditzy and defeated in imitation. "Ever since she confessed, I've been meaning to ask where she slept with him. In a car? In a bed?" Corey reaches up and scissors her cigarette between two fingers and taps a long ash out onto the floor of the garage. "Is it horrible that I'm trying to get a visual? It has to be. It has to be some sort of mental illness."

You look up at the ceiling fan and try to make it speed up telepathically. "My mother didn't sleep with my father until their wedding night," you say. "And he still gave up on her."

"But when?" Corey asks, patting the vacant passenger seat. "Year two or twenty-two? That's the key."

You walk around to the passenger side and get in. The cool leather reaches out for your thighs. The door gives its rich, reassuring *thump*. When *did* your father give up on your mother? Or more importantly: Why is your mother still trying to make him care?

Corey passes you the cigarette. There isn't much left to it. You can taste the taste of filter when you take a drag. "My grandfather saved a bottle of wine for thirty years and when he finally got around to drinking it, it was nothing more than a douche," Corey says. "So, I say, if you want to fuck on the first night, fuck on the first night." Corey takes the butt from your fingers and flicks it out of the car and out into the garage. It arcs up toward the open washing machine and lands in its drum with the muted ding of a dead insect, once again unnerving you and delighting Corey. "Did you see that?" she says, turning to face you. "I just scored."

Corey takes her hands off the wheel and places them on your left thigh. A small but urgent fear rises in you, up from your stomach and into your throat—a single white butterfly looking for light. But you only resist by closing your eyes. For a mild moment, there's nothingness, and then, warm and decisive, Corey is upon you, in a way similar to boys past, but with less neediness, less weight, more conviction. You feel your mouth taken in by Corey's. Your thighs peel away from the leather. Corey moves one of your hands this way, your knees apart that way. You can see: there is an agenda of sorts; there are steps to take. But there is a gentleness involved and you can also see: Corey's mission is based not on consuming but converting.

Soon enough, behind your eyes, you are back on the ferry, looking out at a dark shape in the gray mist. With every move Corey makes, the distant shape sheds some of its darkness and reveals more of itself. A shirt is unbuttoned for a shade of green. A clasp is unclasped for a hint of blue. You taste salt and tobacco. You see the fog lifting, lifting. Before long, your need to see all of the island is so profound that you take over what Corey started. You are the one to press the two of you through the last of the mist, until, for the second time that day, the island appears— bigger and brighter than before. You open your mouth in relief. The butterfly bursts free. It flits from your parted lips and into Corey's. The first thing you see, when you at last open your eyes, is not the medicinal pink of the Porsche or a single curl of smoke rising from the washer, but Corey, beneath you, timid.

This dream has legs. You always think it's over, but there's always PART IV. Sometimes it even says that in the dream, like on a movie screen, a black background with white font: PART IV. PART IV is just an overview of the rest of the summer. That cinematic device called the montage. This is the part of the dream where you see the sun rising every morning at 3:45, the pale blue of another day washing over the futon that you and Corey share. This is where you see you sliding some part of yourself between two parts of Corey, and the two of you waking each other up in a way that melts fog. This is where you see how many islands are within you. There are islands upon islands, chains and keys and archipelagoes. Daily destinations of green and white that burst forth after expanses of tedious mist. This is the part of the dream where you see the ropes that you and Corey pull from the dark sea together, wet knots thumping onto the wood floor of the ship, until your limbs lose power, until all that remains is the lone white butterfly, flitting back and forth.

This is also the part where you see beyond The Engine. A summer of guests with their rented bikes and checkered shirts. Ninety days of the Cliffs, wandering the property midmorning in their keen pants and V-necks. Three months of Quincy shrinking. Three months of the pumpkin growing. There's the curious influx of the town. The local journalist arriving with his clipboard and pumpkin questions. Parents snooping with kids and cameras. That boy from the ferry, that one with the lighter. *Biff.* Here he is again, on the property, whistling impressed at the pumpkin. He's offering to come with a forklift, he's shaking hands with the Cliffs, he's looking side-eyed at Corey who's looking side-eyed at him. This is how the dream always ends. As a nightmare. With you sitting up, alone on the futon in a cold sweat. Waking from a dream within a dream. Knowing that Quincy is gone. That Corey has left. That the pumpkin has split on its driest side to show what it's made of.

Waking up from this dream is always a relief, but always comes with a haze, a daze. You're out of the dream but still in the fog. The dream sticks with you for two or three days, and the only cure seems to be laundry. Only washing and drying and ironing bedsheets for a bed large enough for two people is what melts the fog. Is what talks you off the cliff.

Love Blue

Vi's divorce was final, and Marlo was taking her to the museum and lunch to cheer her up. In Marlo's mind, the outing was a celebration. Good riddance to Allen! She'd never liked him. Allen had bottle-brush eyebrows that he puppeteered around his forehead in false earnestness. Once, at a dinner party, while everyone else was playing charades, Marlo had gone into the kitchen for tonic and discovered Allen eating a baked potato over the kitchen sink, two-handed. "That's what I'm talking about," he said to the potato. "That's more like it."

Allen had always struck Marlo as a fraud, so it was no surprise that fraud was what he was going to fun-jail for. Vi was way better off unmarried, but Marlo couldn't say that out loud. Vi was lovelorn, languishing. She had lost eighteen pounds and was now driving a dented PT Cruiser with advertising wrap on it: *Karmen's Kettle Korn*. Worse still, Vi was giving some New

Age guy free tax prep in exchange for "emotional osteopathy." Vi was so blue she claimed that even her "skin felt dead." So, Marlo had to pretend to sympathize, when really Marlo was pleased. The more single friends Marlo had, the happier she was. She'd been flying solo for more than a decade, and after years of feeling rotten about it, she had come to see herself, and those in her position, as superior. Love, like religion, was for the weak.

"Do you think I need a coat?" Vi asked. They were standing in the foyer of Vi's condo. The condo was bright and marbly and on the market and Vi was bereft about it. "Tell me what I need to bring, Marlo."

Marlo pointed to a poncho. The name of the exhibition was *Where Love Went*, but she didn't tell Vi that. Her plan was to pretend she hadn't known what they were getting into. To be honest, Marlo really didn't know anything about it. She had decided on the exhibition based only on its name, the same way she bet on racehorses. Maybe the exhibition had nothing to do with love. Maybe it was about nuclear weapons. Who cared? If it got bad, they could go down to the museum café and eat over-priced crudités and salted cashews. They could drink sake, talk about wireless bras, Marlo's gum surgery. They could go into the gift shop and buy some glossy space-age salt and pepper shakers the color of cherry tomatoes. Anything was better than staying at home and standing in Allen's closet, staring at his white-collar shirts.

"The museum will get your mind off things," Marlo said. "That's why they made museums."

Vi put on the coat that Marlo held out. "I've never understood art," she said.

*

It was a rainy fall day. Not too cold. The streets were shiny silver, and here and there on the sidewalk were yellow and orange leaves, dropped like children's mittens. There were puddles tinged with gasoline, giant thumbprints of moonstone. Marlo thought it was delightful. She and Vi were both dressed in black coats and carried black umbrellas and Marlo thought they looked like witches. What witch spent too much time pining for a man who ate a potato with two hands? Still, Vi looked miserable. Did she even see the double-decker bus with the soggy tourists? The wincing Chihuahua paralyzed by his rain boots? Marlo didn't think so, and it was a shame; their misery was comedic.

"Oh, great," Vi said when they reached the museum. It had been recently redone and was the size of a regional airport. Its steel and fiberglass gave off a sterile, government-funded optimism. "*Where Love Went*. Did you plan this, Marlo? I'm going to kill you."

"Well, look at that," Marlo lied, eyeing the hot-pink banner. "Maybe we can learn something."

The two women entered, obedient as schoolgirls. They closed and shook their umbrellas under the awning. They checked their coats and tucked the numbered stubs in their wallets, then tucked their wallets in their crossbodies. They bought their full-price tickets and waited, without fidgeting, for the elevator to arrive.

"I don't require a headset," Vi said. "I'd rather feel dumb on my own time."

"You're not dumb," Marlo said, but she said it because she felt she had to. She was starting to feel sorrier for herself than for Vi. Maybe Allen had committed fraud because Vi was so unstimulating. Maybe this outing would be so excruciating that

Marlo would end up eating a potato over her own sink tonight, two-handed.

The exhibition began in a small round room. The walls were painted with a mural of farmland in various shades of blue. At the center of the room was a blue kitchen table. On the table, blue dishes displayed glossy blue apples, a blue roasted turkey, blue string beans, a blue loaf of bread with blue slices falling away.

A recording played on overhead speakers. "In 1957, in the heart of the Wheat Belt," it declared, "Little Tiger Cat Food Company came to the small town of Chaffton and built its world headquarters. All of Little Tiger's buildings were painted a distinct shade of blue known as Love Blue. The company's fleet of trucks, also all painted Love Blue, clogged the prairie town's roads. The company donated a Little League ballpark with Love Blue bleachers. It built a Love Blue-bricked opera house. A Love Blue-tiled waterpark. Little Tiger even offered free Love Blue fencing to any household in need of a fence. After the 1962 tornado, it replaced the town's roofs with Love Blue shingles. In 1963, the town was renamed Love Blue. By 1965, Love Blue had the highest suicide rate in the plains states. Love Blue also had the highest teen pregnancy rate and the highest divorce rate in the state. Love Blue, the color, fell somewhere between cyan and cadet. It had been formulated by a World War II psychiatrist who based it off the eye color of his pet Siberian husky, Fyodor."

Marlo and Vi watched as a blue family inflated before their eyes at the blue kitchen table. A father expanded. A mother with a beehive hairstyle put on pounds with a gentle hiss. A balloon boy, in a light-blue-and-dark-blue striped shirt, extended a fat hand toward a glass of blue milk. A plump daughter, clearly an airhead, stared blankly at her bowl of blue soup.

"Everything tastes blue," a girl's voice said overhead.

"Everything smells blue," a boy's voice said.

"I love blue," a man's voice said.

"I am blue," a woman's voice said.

The recording went on to play the clinking sounds of dinnertime. To Marlo, blue forks and blue spoons and blue knives sounded more intolerable than stainless ones. After some time, the blue family slowly deflated and the lights came on. When Marlo and Vi exited the round room, an attendant handed them each a small blue card the size of cracker. On its reverse side it said: *YOU ARE LOVED.*

Vi read the card and sighed. "Was," she said.

Marlo wanted to say something snide, but instead she slid the card into a side pocket of her crossbody like a secret wish. She thought about the blue town. About everyone trying to escape its predictability through sex and death, affairs and babies. The cause of bad behavior was always monotony, monogamy. Marlo had learned this the hard way. The whole world was painted Love Blue if you looked at it right.

"What if I run into him here?" Vi was still holding the card. She didn't have the self-respect to hide it like Marlo had. "What if, as his last hurrah before jail, he's here? Wandering around? Allen. It's something he would do."

Marlo snatched the card from Vi and offered it back like a parking ticket. "Put this in your pocket, will you?" She looked around for the next exhibit. "Allen is drinking a martini somewhere. Eating a Wagyu steak. He's not the answer, Vi. Especially not now."

Vi took the card but did not put it away. "You know, Marlo.

Unlike you, I happen to believe in love. I say: 'Better to be lost in love than to have never tried to lose.'"

Marlo stopped in her tracks and shook her head. "That's not how it goes, Vi. Not the saying, not life. And especially not love."

In the second room, doll-sized coffins were hung from the ceiling with fishing wire. They were all painted high-gloss black and propped open to reveal red-velvet insides where doilies were pinned with hat pins.

"Oh boy," Vi said. "This one is going to be a doozy."

Marlo squinted. She walked toward a swaying coffin and put her hands on her hips. Her determination to interpret the art was growing with Vi's bewilderment. "*BUTTERCUPS*," read Marlo. "And this one says *MY PET CHICKENS HERO AND PECKY*. What does that one say, Vi?" Marlo pointed.

Vi stood on tiptoes. "*MY HAND BETWEEN MY LEGS*," she said. "Is it vulgar or funny? I mean, please don't tell me it can be both at the same time."

Marlo moved on like she knew the answer and read the coffins silently to herself. *SALT AND OIL. DIGGING WITH A STICK IN THE AUTUMN DIRT. THE LOOK ON MY FATHER'S FACE BEFORE HE SNEEZED. A FINISHED MATH PROBLEM. A LIFESAVER SUCKED DOWN TO A TINY RED GLASS RING. WHEN CHURCH IS OVER. THAT ONE GENTLE SUMMER MONDAY IN THE TOYS "R" US PARKING LOT. YOUR SAD SOFT STOMACH OVERHANGING THE WAIST OF YOUR FAVORITE PANTS AND YOU NOT FEELING LIKE YOU HAVE TO BE SELF-CONSCIOUS IN FRONT OF ME. COLD MUSHROOM SOUP IN THE BACK OF MY GRANDMOTHER'S HARVEST GOLD FRIDGE.*

Marlo stood and stared. A feeling rose in her. It began as nostalgia, then morphed into a wave of grief, then a wave of anguish. For an instant, Marlo remembered fondness, which was too close to remembering love, which was really no different than remembering tragedy. The coffins swayed . . . or was it Marlo? She caught a whiff of funeral lilies. Was she going to go there? To that place she had gotten really good at not going? Yes, apparently, she was. She was going to go back to her old bedroom. *Their* bedroom. To the doorway and his silhouette over her silhouette. To Marlo watching the silhouettes, too mortified, too betrayed to interrupt. Eventually she'd gone out to her car. *Where Love Went.* That was where love had gone. Out to a sangria-colored Jeep Cherokee. Thank God there hadn't been a gun in the glove box. If there had been a gun it would have gone into Marlo's mouth. Or maybe first to the back of his head and then second to the front of whoever she was's head and then third in Marlo's mouth. Would there have been a chance Marlo would have spared herself?

"I think this exhibit is about all the good things that have died," Vi said. "I think I get it! I think I can relate! Think about all the things you've loved, Marlo, that have died, been buried."

"I'd rather not," Marlo managed.

"Well, I like this!" Vi gave a little smile of renewal. "I think this speaks to me! Maybe I'll go out of this world with all sorts of coffins filled with all sorts of old loves." Vi gave a short, satisfied sniff. "This was a great idea," she said. "This museum. Really, Marlo."

Marlo glowered. She felt like day drinking. She moved on to the next room without comment. On the wall hung an oversized canvas painted black. If Marlo stood too close, she couldn't see anything but the color black, but if she stood further back, where the heart stickers were stuck on the floor, where the other patrons had begun to gather, she could see there were letters painted beneath the black paint. It seemed the letters were also painted in black, but perhaps in a different texture or direction. Marlo could make out a *D* and an *E*. She couldn't say if she saw a *T* or an *F*.

"What does it say?" she asked a woman next to her. Her voice sounded uncharacteristically forlorn. "Can you see what it says?"

The woman shrugged and moved away. Now the feeling was rising, rising in Marlo. She had to bite her tongue, clench her buttocks. She'd felt this way at Vi's wedding, as the maid of honor, right when Vi had walked down the aisle. *Don't pass out,* she'd told herself. *Don't throw up.* Vi had been so beautiful. So innocent in her silly tulle. So full of faith that everything would turn out okay. Marlo could have told her otherwise. Marlo gave the black canvas a good long stare until the *T* could also pass for an *I*. Until her anxiety could pass for terror. Then Vi was there, standing behind Marlo. Marlo could sense her presence, her warmth. It was as if the exhibit were filling Vi up with joy and energy, height even, while Marlo was swaying, shrinking, melting.

"I've had enough," Marlo said, still facing the painting. "It's all obscure for the sake of obscurity. I don't see how this is doing you any good whatsoever. This is no place for the heartbroken." Marlo sniffed. Her limbs were gelatinous. "I need food," she announced. "I'm going down to the café to spend more money than I should on salted cashews just to get away from this nonsense."

Marlo sped through the three remaining rooms of the exhibition in a cold sweat. From what she could tell in her haste, one room was filled knee-deep with empty takeout containers, another played a slideshow of roadkill. In the final room, Marlo went briskly past a yellow synthetic car sponge on a pedestal. Another overhead recording played, but the only word Marlo could make out at her speed was *PANCREATIC*.

"Absurd," she muttered. "Insulting." Now, she was out into the hall with Vi at her back. She went into the stairwell and down one flight, her footsteps clomping like a loose, panicked horse, Vi's clipping along behind her. At the third-floor landing, Marlo felt close to hyperventilating. She stopped at the fire door and clutched its lever, panting. Then she turned around to face Vi, who turned out to not be Vi at all. Instead it was a man. A strange and unexpected man in a blue shirt and blue pants— smiling. Earnest.

"Oh . . ." Marlo wheezed. Her heart was really worked up now. How it was keeping her alive made less sense than anything in the museum.

"I'm Dex," the man said in a way that sounded apologetic. "The artist." He held out his hand to Marlo, but Marlo just looked down at it. The man's fingernails were painted the color of a chlorinated pool.

Is that Love Blue? Marlo thought to herself.

"This is Love Blue," the artist said, admiring his nails. "The one and only." Dex gave up on a formal handshake and dropped his hand to his side. He nodded at the fire door with his head. His hair was parted, wet and perfect as a child's. "I could tell the exhibition was really doing a number on you. I was afraid you might faint. Believe it or not, I've seen people faint. I like to get a reaction out of my visitors, but going unconscious is never the goal. Why don't I buy you lunch? Could I buy you lunch?"

Marlo let her breath return. She *was* famished. And cheap. *Why not?* she thought. She didn't know him, but they'd be in public, safe. In her mind, she saw a little coffin, suspended, and inside it a doily that read: *GOING IT ALONE*. After a moment, Marlo exhaled. She pointed to the door lever and nodded.

In the café, Dex ordered two glasses of sake. And a little cobalt bowl of smoked almonds. He also requested a plate of crudités, which came to the table, damp and vivid, in all different colors, carrots mostly: wine red, bruise purple, gleeful yellow. All of them had been curled by some darling device that created a platter of energetic tendrils. An explosion of edible streamers. Surprise.

"You know. To catch a rabbit, you don't chase a rabbit," Dex said. He made bunny ears with his fingers and bounced them over to the plate of vegetables and pretended to sniff. "I haven't been on a date in eleven years."

Marlo drank her sake in one gulp. It tasted like an overripe banana. Her heart was nearing normal. What was Vi thinking up there in the exhibition? Was she just standing, staring at picture after picture of wounded raccoons, thinking about Allen? Was she thinking about her condo, its view, the cool feel of its marble under her bare feet? About how someone else would walk into her kitchen in a few months and say *How did I get so lucky?*

Marlo looked at Dex and Dex looked at Marlo. She wanted him to answer all her questions, but she knew she'd have to ask them first. Instead, Marlo just said, "Twelve. It's been twelve for me."

I'm Your Venus

On the bad winter of 1994, Minerva awoke at three in the morning during the fourth blizzard and pulled her suitcase out from under my bed. "Your bed" is what she called it even though we'd been sharing it for six months—longer than Minerva had been with anyone else exclusively. She slept around. Not in a sexual way, but in a let-me-hold-you-while-you-cry sort of way. She was the village witch that tended to the village idiots. Her business card said *Minerva Lamplighter: Professional Spooner. Soothsayer. Doom-Slayer.* She'd been in the bed of most every local man between the ages of twenty-five and seventy-five, curled up behind them, saying: "Now, now. There, there. Mommy's here. Tell your troubles to Mama." She didn't like her job. She wanted to be a carpenter. But the Universe had other plans for her.

"Jesus didn't want to be a carpenter, and I didn't want to be Jesus. But here we are. We do what we're called to do."

I admired her for that. Envied her, actually. I was a fifty-two-year-old math teacher at the community college. I drank enough SKYY vodka every night to kill a better man. I ate cold pizza for breakfast, right out of my hands, while I stared out of my glass front door at the crows. I had gingivitis, gastritis, empty eyes the color of pencil lead. I had a dead wife named Maeve who I'd never even loved, and I was obligated to spend one afternoon a week with her son from a previous marriage doing the sorts of things I assumed stepdads did. Making tough steaks on a grill I had trouble operating. Throwing a football heartlessly back and forth. The kid's name was Justice and he had dreadlocks. My name was Dave and I had a receding hairline. I'm pretty sure I was the worst thing to ever happen to him. I know I'm the worst thing to ever happen to me.

But anyway, Minerva pulled out the suitcase while the snow was blowing insane outside, like sifted flour through a fan. She found her bikini in a drawer and put it in the suitcase, which was really not a suitcase, but a little fireproof safe that most people bought for deeds and wills.

"A bikini?" I said. "That's it? That's all?"

Minerva twisted the combination on the safe, opened it up and put the bikini inside. The bikini was a flimsy thing, a wad of yellow strings. A plate of spaghetti I'd like to see spilled on her. "Where I'm going, even this'll be too much," she said.

"Where on earth are you going?" I said. "A nudist colony? Ecuador?"

Minerva shut the safe and tucked it under her arm. "I'm going nowhere on earth," she said. "I'm going to Venus. The planet." She kissed me on the forehead like the mother she was. "It's hot as balls there, if you didn't know. And now I've told you, so now you do."

*

With Minerva gone, I resorted to my worst and earlier ways. To my original sins. To what I did between Maeve's funeral and me finding Minerva's business card under my windshield wiper. I went down to Don's, the bar, and took the stool at the west end. Don, the eponymous owner, didn't flinch when I sat down, though it had been 179 days since my last visit. Don didn't even take my order. He just filled up a shot glass with hot SKYY and filled up a beer glass with warm Guinness and slid them both in front of me like Thanksgiving dinner.

"Dave," he said.

"Don," I said.

When I'd had four of each, I stumbled over to Frenzy's, the pizza place, where the manager, Nate, was fielding calls from the college kids and townies. He still had his broom-colored ponytail low and loose at the base of his skull, his stained apron, his furrowed brow, the cordless phone tucked under his chin. His hands, veined and coarse from manual labor, from the demands of dough, were still the hands of an old man. His hands looked eighty, even though Nate was only twenty-four. I sat at his counter like I'd sat at Don's, and Nate served me without taking my order as Don had. He slid two slices of Hawaiian under my nose, followed by a plastic container of ranch.

"Dave," he said.

"Nate," I said.

Nate, like Minerva, had also answered a vocational call with a fury I could not conjure, could not fathom. While I chewed and swallowed, I watched him work. In life, it seemed, there were dough and doers, there were the needy and the kneady. I fell into the first of both categories. I was soft *and* helpless. The more I watched Nate work, the more I loved him. The more I watched Nate work, the more I hated myself. I saw me spooning Nate and Minerva spooning me. I saw myself weak and crying between them. The purposeless between the purposeful. Old meat between holy bread.

"My whole life is about circles," Nate had once said. "Pizzas, pepperonis, onion slices, pineapple rings. See this slicer?" He'd pointed to the big stainless steel machine behind him. "When it goes, I go."

I remembered this as Nate got a call for six Italian grinders. I watched him slice circles of salami, circles of pale watery ham, circles of provolone, circles of ruffled iceberg. My heart broke as I watched. I could feel it in Nate's hands, my sliced heart, with every back-and-forth of the machine. It was all I could do not to sob. What good was a man like me? I asked Nate to wrap the rest of my pizza. I stood and thanked him. He was on the phone. He was hard at work. I tipped him a twenty. He didn't even notice. That night, I slept fitfully. I dreamed I looked through a telescope and saw a bikini dangling from a crescent moon. I dreamed Nate made Minerva a wooden pizza that she cut with a saw. I dreamed I was dough, kneaded beyond rising. I dreamed I was sick, over a toilet, and all that came up were circles: red, yellow, green, purple.

In the morning, I ate the remaining ham and provolone off a leftover Italian grinder in the fridge while I stood and watched the winter crows out my glass front door. They arrived in the white yard like men in black business suits, commuters between trains. They strutted about in the snow like they weren't expecting anything. Like they could give or take all or nothing. Minerva had once told me that birds liked shiny things. Winter crows especially. That they collected coins and tinsel and foil wrappers and decorated their nests with them. That there was nothing they loved more. I went and found my pants on the bedroom floor. I took some nickels from the pocket. I went outside in my slippers and robe and the crows leaped away—disgusted, not scared—and I scattered the coins on top of the hard snow. Back inside, I waited at the door for the crows to return, but the crows had moved on to whiter pastures. In the bright morning sun, the nickels looked happy. I pretended I had done one good thing with my time.

Minerva was gone for a week. When she returned, she was tan, the color of maple syrup, and she carried a tote bag that said *What Happens on Venus Stays on Venus*.

"I brought you something," she said. She dug around in the tote bag and pulled out a snow globe. Inside of it were a bunch of tiny women the color of maple syrup and dressed in yellow bikinis, holding hands in a circle around a volcano. Instead of snow, orange glitter rained down on them. "Venus." Minerva shook her head in awe. "What a ride, what a ride."

"What else is in the bag?" I asked.

Minerva held the bag close to her body. "It's all volcanic, all women. Gals and gas. Sorority and sulfur. Well, there's one guy there, Maxwell Montes. I know. Only one guy? You're thinking: he must be the king of Venus! But, no. You're wrong. He's our toy."

"A sex slave?" I said. "What's in the bag?"

"Your word choice is off," Minerva said. "The cure." She touched the bag. "That's what's in the bag."

"The cure for what?" I asked.

"For what ails you."

Minerva was only home for five days. In that time, she held me ten times and I cried eight of them. She praised me for my progress. She shook out the bed linens. She burned sage. She made her mushroom teas. She lined up her seven rainbow glasses on the windowsill and let the sunlight make chakra water. She made me gargle the water. The indigo nearly killed me. Minerva made me hold quartz crystals and talk about Maeve and math, two things I felt nothing for. At meals, she stirred my soup counterclockwise and her soup clockwise. She put her hands above my head and clapped. I just watched her, admired her, hated her. Her glossy coal mane, her decisive face, the ease she oozed.

"It's the midlife," she said. "It's got you bad."

"How do I get rid of it?" I asked. I was desperate.

"Try or die," Minerva said. "Try or die," she repeated.

I hated her because she was right. I hated her because she knew she was right. I hated her because I hated myself. I hated myself because I hated her. How did she even get to Venus? Amtrak? LSD? Teleportation? I wanted to know, but I couldn't muster the energy to ask. It's not like I was allowed there anyway.

When the snow returned, the safe came back out from under the bed, *my bed*, and the bikini went inside of it and Minerva went off a second time. I looked everywhere for the tote bag while she was gone. I hadn't seen her leave with it, but I couldn't find it. Maybe she'd put it in the safe. Maybe I'd imagined it. I missed her terribly. I didn't know what to do with myself when she was gone. I didn't know what to do with myself when she was here, either, but when she was here, she was at least trying to fix me.

Every afternoon of Minerva's absence, I went down to Don's, and every night, I closed out the day at Frenzy's. On Mondays, Wednesdays, and Fridays I taught Finite Math at the community college. The kids watched me teach with the enthusiasm of the dead. I taught them nothing they'd ever use. They knew it and I knew it. It was like singing a lullaby to rocks. On Tuesdays, Justice came by for his overcooked steak and baked potato. It had grown too cold for football, so after dinner, I'd make him listen to *Exile on Main St.* One night, before he left, I rummaged through a dresser drawer and pulled out an old *Penthouse* and handed it to him. He held up his hands and took two steps backward, refusing to touch it, but I went on and opened up the magazine and let the centerfold unfold. I figured a stepdad had to do what a stepdad had to do, but Justice closed his eyes and shook his head and left. On that particular night, I went down to Don's and had five vodkas and five beers, and on that particular night, instead of eating anything at Frenzy's, I sat in the parking lot, in an empty, unlocked car that I was pretty sure was Nate's, and I waited for Nate to finish his work. I went in and out of what I thought was sleep, but I was so cold, so drunk, it was hard to tell. At some point, Nate got into the car and I scared him. Not on purpose, just my presence.

"Man," Nate said. "You scared me."

"Show me where you live," I said. "Show me how you live."

"What?" Nate asked. "Show you how to live?"

"That too," I said. "Where you live and how you live and how *to* live."

Nate said okay. I could tell: he was a worker in every way. Not just at Frenzy's. He was assignment-oriented. A tasker. He did what was asked of him. He didn't strike me as particularly smart, just industrious. I could tell he would have liked Finite Math. He would have made me feel like I was contributing something to society. I saw his face in my classroom. I saw his face in the glow of the moon. He started the car.

"Aren't you freezing?" he said. "Because you could have frozen to death out here."

"Have you ever been to Venus?" I asked.

"What's Venus?" he said. "A restaurant?"

"It's a planet," I said.

"Oh," he said. "Then no."

Nate's car wasn't much. It was some old two-door that shuddered and whistled in the cold night.

"There's a hole in my floorboard," he said. "Down by your feet."

I looked down, but I couldn't see anything. I couldn't feel anything. I couldn't speak.

"I think you need to warm up," Nate said. "What were you thinking?"

Nate's house was a little red rental with a purple porch light. Nate helped me out of the car. His girlfriend met us at the door. Her name was Nicole, and she had on a tank top. She had large breasts with wings tattooed on them. There was some makeup smudged under her eyes. Behind her, I could make out a blurry kitchenette, a leather couch, a glass bong.

"He doesn't look good," she said to Nate. Her face was scared. "Is he okay?"

Nate had two strong hands on me. One clamping each shoulder. "He's drunk and cold," he said. "And maybe stupid. But we can fix him. You and me."

Nate and Nicole put a comforter on the leather couch. They

put me on the comforter. They put a blanket on me and then Nate climbed behind me and held me, and Nicole laid on top of both of us.

"This'll do," Nate said.

I felt myself thaw. I felt Nicole's breasts and Nate's breath. "What good is a man like me?" I whispered. "What good am I in the world?"

"He needs something to eat," Nicole said to Nate.

"Am I at the beginning or the end?" I said. "The circle of life. Where on it am I?"

"I'll heat up some slices," Nate said to Nicole.

I didn't want him to leave me.

"I'll do it," Nicole said.

I didn't want her to leave me either.

"Tell me I'm either at the very beginning," I said, "or the very end." Nate and Nicole both sat up. They tucked the blanket around me. "I either need more time or no more time."

Then I was quiet. They were quiet. They left me. I heard them in the kitchen. I heard a timer ding, and I smelled pizza getting warm. I was getting warm. I fell asleep. I opened my eyes at one point and saw Nicole take off her tank top. Her nipples were as brown as maple syrup. She walked out of the room. At another point, I heard the sounds of sex, but I couldn't open my eyes no matter how hard I tried. In the morning, I heard another timer ding. I saw Nate walk by the couch. He was naked. His uncircumcised penis flopped as he walked, like a wet sock between his legs. He made life look easy. He moved about with more than confidence, he moved about with relevance. When I woke up a final time, Nate and Nicole were gone. I folded the comforter and the blanket and sat for a while with my face in my hands. When I quit doing that, I found a note and a set of keys on the dining table. Nate had left his car for me to drive to my house, but I was too embarrassed to see him again for a while. I'd have to get drunk all over again to face him when he picked his car up. So, I went outside and walked around the little red rental to think. In the snow under Nate's bedroom window were four used condoms. Red, yellow, green, purple. Circles unfolding. I wondered if they were all from one night. When was the last time it snowed? I was equally amazed and depressed.

I decided to hitchhike without using my thumb. I walked along the main road until a man in a truck slowed down and gave me a ride. He didn't talk and I didn't talk, and it was starting to feel like one kind thing after another. When I got home, I shook the snow globe until I shook all the women loose from the bottom and they floated at the top. I was trying to get Minerva back home.

Minerva eventually came home on her own time. This time, she was as tan as French roast and smelled of sulfur. Like old eggs with fresh insides.

"I'm hot enough to melt lead," she said. Out of her tote bag, she brought out a souvenir spoon, an iron-on Aphrodite patch, and a T-shirt that said *My Girlfriend Went to Venus and All I Got Was This Lousy T-shirt*.

"What about the cure?" I said. "For what ails me?"

Minerva held her tote close to her body. "There's only so much to go around," she said. "There are men much worse off than you, Dave."

I was incredulous. "You can't be serious," I said. "Don't you know me? Can't you see how bad off I am?"

Minerva was unmoved. "What I see," she said, "is how unbecoming all of this is."

I didn't know what to say. I looked at the souvenirs on the kitchen counter. I tried to find the words, but only a single word came to mind: "frenzy."

Minerva sighed a loud sigh. Her breath filled the kitchen with a tangerine haze. "I'm retiring," she said. "I'm done doing what I was asked to do. I'm moving to Venus for good. I'm going to be a carpenter there. Build some decks, some boardwalks by the volcanic fields. Like in Yellowstone. You should go to Yellowstone. Walk on the boardwalks. Get close to the earth's crust. Try or die, Dave. I just came back to get my things."

I hung my head. "It's that Maxwell guy, isn't it?" I asked.

Minerva went over to her little safe on the counter and turned the combination dial. "Of course you think it's a man." Minerva opened the safe and took out her bikini and tossed it to the floor. Then she brought out a little vial and unscrewed its top and picked up the souvenir spoon and filled it with a circle of green liquid. "Open wide," she said to me. "Down the hatch."

I did as directed. It tasted like eggs. Bad ones. I winced, resisted the urge to gag.

"When you get the call," Minerva said. "Pick up." She put the bikini and the vial back into the safe. She started going around the kitchen, collecting her things. It was ending. It was over. I never see anything coming until it's already been gone a while.

Minerva packed her rainbow glasses and her dried mushrooms. She went through my drawers and gathered her scarves and finger cymbals and soap flakes. I couldn't bear to watch her leave, so I left first. I went down to Don's and sat on my stool. I sat there with my warm drinks and waited. I waited for the cure to cure me. I waited to feel better. But instead, the snow picked up outside and it went past the window like Minerva's soap flakes. A television played a silent hockey game. It was all so sad. I was almost too sad to drink. And then, like an antidote, there was Don, in front of me, with the bar telephone, holding out the old dough-colored receiver like a hand extended to a drowning man. Asking me to take the call.

"It's for you," he said, and I put my ear to the phone, but he didn't even have to ask. I knew it was Nate and I knew he needed me to return the favor, all the favors. I knew he was calling for me and only me, and I just said, "Wait. Wait right there. I'm on my way."

I got up from the stool and ran down to Frenzy's, and the run and the snow felt good, exhilarating. I couldn't remember the last time I'd run. When I got to Frenzy's, there was Nate, standing on the deck of the pizza place, holding the big stainless steel slicer like he was holding a wounded woman. For a flash, I saw Nicole, draped in his arms like she needed a ride to the hospital, but then I blinked and it was the slicer. Nate's other love.

"It's in pieces," he said in a voice I'd never heard him use. Was he about to cry? "You have to hold it together while I drive. Hold it together, man. Hold it together."

I reached out for the slicer, and he transferred it to me, and I nearly fell from its weight. Nate went to his car and opened the passenger door and slid the passenger seat all the way back, and I staggered over with the slicer and got in and Nate shut the door. Then we were off, speeding down I-90 in the black night, with the snowflakes whizzing by like stars, and I was in space—we were in outer space.

Nate said nothing, but I could tell he was grateful. He drove faster and faster, past all those cold towns with old names. Past Ilion and Utica, past Rome and Verona. I was ancient. I was relevant. We went speeding down the highway with the silver slicer, with the wind blowing up through the floorboard, and joy washed over me like lava. When the slicer was fixed, I'd let the joy melt me down. I'd let the circular blade of the slicer slice me up, into molten circles, into shiny coins. Nate would drive, and I'd spill out into the night, or the morning, whenever it was, from the floor of the car and out onto the white snow. The birds would have me. They wouldn't be able to resist. They'd pick me up, all my pieces, and take me back to their nests where I would be wanted, worth something. Valuable and chosen. Forever cherished.

Ingrid

The morning after Ingrid set her mattress on fire, she ended up at the mall with a wad of fifties, still wearing pajama bottoms. For two hours prior, she'd aimlessly driven around town hoping to see Oscar's car parked somewhere. She'd cruised past seedy bars, apartment complexes, confronting her husband aloud while she drove. *Well, well, well. What do we have here?* Eventually, Ingrid gave up and, after a stop at an ATM, pulled into the mall parking lot ready to lay down some cash. Inside, the air smelled of treated water and high-fructose corn syrup, and Ingrid moved against shoppers like an upstream salmon—past thundering fountains, past families of headless mannequins—until she reached the mattress store. It was new and sleek and called the Z Spot. Dazed by all the naked kings and queens, Ingrid stood unmoving in its doorway, triggering the automatic chime again and again.

"Can I help you?" a young salesman asked. He touched her elbow gently, moving her one step away from the sensor.

"I doubt it," Ingrid heard herself say.

The salesman looked like a stripper, which Ingrid supposed was a good look if one was selling mattresses. He had brown biceps as large as pumpernickel loaves bursting from his short white sleeves. His black hair was slicked back, as if he'd just gone swimming. His jaw was steely, a game show host's. "You like firm?" he gazed at Ingrid. "What sort of support do you need?"

Ingrid saw a mattress made of concrete on a bed frame made of steel. Would that be enough support given the circumstances? After Oscar had confessed to the affair and after Ingrid had finally gotten him to say the woman's name aloud—*Mindy*—Ingrid had collapsed, sobbing on the kitchen floor for the better part of an hour. During that time, Oscar had gone on to work while Ingrid kept imagining an apple falling from a tree and rolling down a hill. "I'm seeing someone," Oscar kept saying in her mind. And every time she heard his words, the apple would fall and Ingrid would run after it and Oscar would stand off to one side, watching and unburdened, in a grassy corner of Ingrid's mind, while the apple gained speed and disappeared down a hill.

"What are my options?" Ingrid asked the salesman. "I want to know them all."

The salesman flashed a smile it seemed he'd been waiting his whole career to flash. "How long do you have?" he said. "Because we might need to get comfortable first."

After the apple scenario, Ingrid had spent some time on the linoleum considering suicide and homicide and the objects a person could employ for both: box cutters, sleeping pills, fast cars. Then finally, as the last act of her unplanned but well-deserved pity party, Ingrid indulged herself by thinking of all things she'd never done: parasailing, cocaine, plastic surgery, international men. When Ingrid recalled that in college there'd been a Canadian she'd let touch her breasts, the memory functioned like an emotional tourniquet. Her weeping ceased, and she sat up and rubbed her eyes like a child—flushed and finally lucid after a long illness. She stormed out to the patio and retrieved the can of lighter fluid. Then she stormed to the master bedroom and doused the Sealy.

"What about waterbeds?" she asked the salesman. "With mahogany headboards and nightstands attached? Do you have those? Because that's the sort of waterbed I imagine they were on."

The salesman frowned for a moment, then recovered with a wide smile. "You like the motion of the ocean, do you?" His teeth were unnaturally white. Ingrid shaded her eyes. "Come," he said. "Come with me." The salesman led Ingrid to a dim corner of the store and gestured with both arms at a snowy memory foam. "This is our closest thing to a waterbed," he said. "Have at it."

The last time Ingrid had been in a mattress store was with Oscar, twelve years prior, just after their honeymoon on a crowded Carnival cruise they'd made the best of. In the store, they'd bounced on the Sealy side by side, blushing and giddy. They'd had decent enough sex until they'd been unable to have children, then sex had become nothing more than a chore, a joint one. She held the ladder, sullen, while he washed the windows, furious. Through it all, the Sealy had been dependable, even indestructible. Until yesterday. Soaked in butane, it had been no match for the match Ingrid tossed in its center.

Ingrid looked at the salesman and then at the memory foam. She saw Oscar above her with his Windex and squeegee. Ingrid got on the bed and reclined slowly. To her unspoken delight, the salesman proceeded to the opposite side of the mattress and sat down. He swung his feet effortlessly onto the bed and lay beside her. He sighed dramatically, as if he knew and respected the world's sorrows.

"A man came in yesterday," he said. "A trophy hunter. He goes to Africa and pays money to kill giraffes and lions and what are those big buffalo with the horns called?"

"Wildebeest?" Ingrid guessed.

"That sounds right," the salesman said. "My name's Malcolm."

Ingrid thought to say *Hello, Malcolm* or *Nice to meet you*, but she did not.

"He said he needed a better mattress, but I knew what he needed was to talk." Malcolm clasped his hands over his stomach and waited.

Ingrid stalled. She saw the match flutter on the quilted surface, the Sealy momentarily wield its flame-retardant shield, the master bedroom promptly fill with a dense green smoke that smelled somewhere between crème brûlée and singed hair. Ingrid saw herself call 9-1-1, make a cup of tea, sit on her front stoop, wave at neighbors. She saw the neighbors stop and gape as the smoke, now black and roiling, poured from a window. Ingrid had waited blankly, patiently, for the people who would come and try to undo what she'd done. What did they call them now? *First responders.*

"'Jesus Henry,'" Ingrid finally said. The salesman said nothing. "That's what Oscar said when he came home and saw what I'd done. 'Jesus Henry and Christ on a bike!' He was a devout Catholic, you know, until the whole infertility mess, so

116

I could see I'd gotten to him. I'm not without talent." Ingrid thought about how to catch Malcolm up to speed. "I set the mattress on fire. The bedroom ceiling fan melted into a hard, white knuckle. It was a fan Oscar had had a terrible time installing. 'Why on earth would you go and do this?' he had the nerve to say to me. 'I didn't even sleep with her in our godforsaken bed, Ingrid. I slept with her on a waterbed.'"

Ingrid felt certain she knew what the waterbed looked like. It had the mahogany headboard, maroon sheets. On the built-in bedside tables there were definitely two glasses of cheap sherry. Barbra Streisand, who Ingrid hated and Oscar adored, was most certainly playing from Oscar's phone. And Mindy was no doubt vocal and dramatic, a good actress. It was likely she was not pretty—because Oscar wasn't pretty—but it was certain Mindy was willing, because Ingrid no longer was.

"Anyway," Ingrid said. "I'm here because I burn beds, unlike the other guy you mentioned. The trophy hunter. I don't murder giraffes, but I might murder her."

Malcolm went on as if she'd never said a thing. "Trust me: I see it all. A man came in on Tuesday and told me all about the Southern Baptists and what they'd done to him. On Wednesday, a college kid lifted his shirt and showed me his colostomy bag. And, last Thursday, a woman lay right where you are and told me about a car wreck where a baby had landed in the street and was quite clearly dead but was still smiling."

Ingrid imagined Mindy's stomach swollen with a baby, then two babies, then triplets.

Malcolm went on. "What's her name? That's a key detail."

"Mindy," Ingrid said. "What else would it be?"

Malcolm turned toward Ingrid. He propped himself up on

one elbow and looked at her. Ingrid still lay on her back facing upward. There had been seven miscarriages in all, each one so devastating to Ingrid that Oscar had once suggested naming them after the Seven Dwarfs to provide some levity. She should have seen that as the beginning of the end, or the actual end, but she had given Oscar a forced smile and gone easy on him for this absurd suggestion. The fertility specialist had told her men felt helpless in situations of infertility and it was her job to make Oscar feel virile.

"We couldn't make a child so we couldn't make it work," Ingrid sighed. "The marriage, that is." Malcolm did not speak. He was waiting and Ingrid didn't want to disappoint. "'Fecund' was the word the doctor used. 'Make your husband feel *fecund*.' What a disgusting word, but—no surprise—the specialist himself was disgusting. He was an arrogant brute with clumsy hands and a turkey baster. I saw him once outside the office. He was driving an orange Audi and playing the Allman Brothers with the windows down. He was wearing a giant silver watch that was so big I thought it was an alarm clock on his wrist." Ingrid snorted. "He didn't even know the words to 'Ramblin' Man.' Who doesn't know the words to 'Ramblin' Man?' What a fraud!"

Ingrid's voice cracked. Malcolm lay back down from his elbow and stared at the ceiling. This felt like camaraderie, so Ingrid cleared her throat and pressed on. "The Seven Dwarfs," she gave a high, false laugh. "'Happy,' Oscar would say after a few drinks. 'Sleepy, Dopey, Bashful.' He could never name more than four. He was naming the babies, Malcolm. Our lost children, after dwarfs. Who does that? A psychopath? A sociopath? What's the difference between the two, because I can never remember."

For a good while there was only the distant sound of the mall fountains. Last night, following the mattress fire, Oscar had slept on the couch. He'd used his coat for a blanket like their house was a city park. He even wore his shoes. Ingrid, on the other hand, did not sleep at all. The whole house smelled of camp-fire and wet carpet, the end of something monumental. She'd gone into the guest room and taken her wedding dress out of its storage box. She'd put on the dress as best she could, which was only to her thick waist, then she fell back on the guest room bed, wearing the dress as a skirt and her practical bra on top. After that, she'd said a prayer that went something like: "Please let Mindy be unable to have children. Or, if Mindy is able to have children, please let the children hate her."

Malcolm finally spoke. "Sometimes life is about the things we don't have instead of the things we do," he said. "Which is difficult."

Ingrid felt heard. "We weren't just seeing the fertility doctor. We were also seeing a marriage counselor. She was a woman, which was hard for Oscar; he felt ganged up on even though she was nice to him. She told me and Oscar, 'You two need to go on vacation. Ingrid is a hen who needs relaxation to lay her eggs. She can probably only conceive in hotels or on beaches. Chalets, maybe. Motor inns.' So, that's what we did, Malcolm. We went on an all-inclusive vacation to 'facilitate ovulation,' and, oh, what a waste it was."

It had taken three long flights on three hot planes to get to an island that looked no different than Key West. The hotel room had damp, pink carpet. There was a lone, giant pool with dated tile and shrunken complimentary towels, and, of course, the macaroni kid.

"On the first day of our so-called ovulation vacation we go to the pool and not five minutes later Oscar says to me: 'Watch this kid, Ingrid. Watch his gall.' Then he yanks out my earbud right there at the pool. I remember I was listening to orca sounds. Oh, God. Those sounds. The clicking and moaning. They were supposed to calm me down but they did the exact opposite. Anyway, Oscar yanks out my earbud and points to this kid. He's drinking a daiquiri. Oscar is, not the kid. I wasn't supposed to drink because the going opinion was that it would lower my chances of conception. But anyway, Oscar is drinking and pointing to this boy."

Ingrid remembered the child with a strange fondness. She'd sat there in her skirted bathing suit with her left earbud dangling. She already had the body and mind of a mother because of the prescribed hormones—thick waist, thick thighs, thick emotions, thick thinking. The boy stood in the shallow end, fuming at a man and a woman in lounge chairs.

"Macaroni!" he shouted. "Macaroni! Macaroni! Macaroni!" The man and woman wore large, insect-like sunglasses and did nothing. Next to the man was a sweaty six-pack of beer. Next to the woman, a collection of pool toys still in their netted bag from the store. "Macaroni!" the boy insisted, stomping the water. "Macaroni! Macaroni! Macaroni!"

Ingrid turned on the memory foam to Malcolm. She raised up on her elbow this time and faced him. "Oscar couldn't handle it. 'That brat has said 'macaroni' twenty-two times,' he said. 'If no one says something soon, I'm going over there and giving that kid a piece of my mind.' And I was like, 'Oh, Oscar. Maybe something's wrong with him.' Which I didn't really believe, but I felt like that was something a woman who wanted a baby might say. And Oscar goes: 'He's not retarded, Ingrid. He's the other

R-word. Rotten.' And when Oscar said 'retarded' and I didn't say anything back, that's when I realized I was done. That's when I realized I just wanted to feel unbroken. I think I actually sat there watching the boy and saw myself get pregnant and give the baby away. I was glad about it. In my head, I told the person I gave the baby to that I'd pay for a year's supply of formula and even assemble the crib. Just take it! Here!"

Ingrid stayed up on her elbow and gazed out into the mall. People milled about like emotionless movie extras. On that same trip, on the flight down, Oscar let Ingrid know that he didn't want just one child, but at least two. "Only children are a cross all of humanity has to bear," Oscar said. "There's only one only child and that's Christ."

Maybe that had been Ingrid's breaking point and not the *R*-word. Maybe realizing she'd have to conceive and carry, not once but twice, was what had done her in. Her whole life would be about hoping not to bleed.

"So," Malcolm asked. "Did the boy get his macaroni?"

Ingrid felt a jolt of adoration. "Oh, yes," she said. "He got his macaroni. He had to say 'macaroni' fifty-three times, but eventually his mother got up and went to the pool bar and came back with a red bowl. She made a big production out of it. She held up that red bowl and announced, 'Look, Lucas! Macaroni and cheese!' And everyone at the pool stared at that bowl like it was a blood moon. But, no surprise, the kid was having none of it. He came marching out of the pool like a little soldier." Ingrid sat up on the bed to illustrate. She swung her arms at her sides and frowned. "'I said macaroni! Not macaroni *and cheese*!' And then he takes the bowl and stares into it and everyone at the pool starts groaning like they've been stabbed. Except me. I'm cheering at this point. On the inside, at least. 'Plain macaroni!' the boy shouts and it's all I can do to not jump up from my pool chair and say, 'You tell 'em, kid!' But I don't. I sit there like everyone else and I watch as the kid holds out the macaroni and cheese, cranks back his little leg, and drop-kicks the bowl like he's at soccer practice."

A smile spread across Malcolm's face. Ingrid felt renewed. What had happened last night? What had happened this morning? "And the bowl goes up, up, up," Ingrid continued, "and then it comes down, down, down and it crashes between two teenage girls in bikinis and macaroni goes everywhere and Lucas starts screaming, 'My foot! My foot! It's broken! I broke it!' And I just start shaking all over with laughter. I'm imagining how horrible the kid would be in a cast. I'm seeing him on crutches. He'd end his parents' marriage! They'd wonder why they'd ever tried so hard to conceive. 'What was the reason again?' they'd ask themselves. And then they'd just give up and get divorced, because they would never be able to remember the reason."

Ingrid lay back down beside Malcolm. Something stirred in her stomach. What if she were finally pregnant? What if Oscar's child grew inside of her like a punch line? The joke would be on her. Would she be able to laugh?

"The night of macaroni kid, I had two rum punches at dinner. Oscar was afraid I would kill my eggs, and I told him, 'Only the bad ones,' and he didn't think that was funny at all. He gave me the silent treatment all through dinner, so when we got back to the hotel room, I locked myself in the bathroom and flushed my Clomid down the toilet. Clomid is a fertility drug," Ingrid explained. "It's supposed to make your ovaries release lots and lots of eggs, but all it ever released for me was lots and lots of guilt."

At the front of the Z Spot, the chime announced a new customer. Malcolm sat up on cue and smoothed his shirt. He swung his feet back over the edge of the memory foam. "The worst feeling in the world isn't guilt. It's not even grief. It's love. Love causes guilt and grief. Love is the antagonist."

Malcolm got up. Ingrid continued to stare at the ceiling. She tried to think about love as the enemy, but all she could see was the Clomid going down the drain, into the water system, and out to sea. She saw fish drink it in through their gills and grow fatter than fat with caviar. She saw herself at the sort of party she never got invited to, celebrating something big. Not a baby, not a wedding, but maybe a promotion. Ingrid saw herself eat the caviar on toast points with sour cream. *Well done*, people told her. *Bravo!*

Ingrid got up. Malcolm was at the front of the store, smiling his blinding smile at the new customer.

"I don't need a bed after all," Ingrid announced.

"Well, I'm here if you change your mind," Malcolm said. "And I'm here if you don't."

Ingrid set off on a brisk walk. She passed a whoopee cushion sale at Mr. Stupid, a pair of novelty goldfish boots at Shake Your Booty, fluorescent yellow overalls in the window of Queen B. At the airbrushing kiosk, SprayBaby, Ingrid paused to admire the license plates and cropped tees—all recklessly romantic, all shamelessly emblazoned with the bright names of loved ones. *Donnie. Roni. Angel. Kitty.* Pink, purple, gold. Sunset, dolphin, puffy heart. Ingrid could not imagine such neon worship.

Ingrid resumed her speed walk. She walked until she was able to see how Malcolm was right. How love caused guilt and how love caused grief and how love was to blame for everything.

She walked until she saw Malcolm's pumpernickel arms cradling a baby—the dead, smiling baby from his car-wreck story. She walked until she saw the macaroni kid with his macaroni and then Oscar with a Hefty bag, coming to gather a few beloved belongings—the handheld telescope that didn't work, the glass paperweight with the real scorpion inside. Would he speak to her as he filled the bag? Would Ingrid speak to him? Ingrid couldn't say. All she could do was power her way to the north end of the mall to a popular restaurant called Monday, Monday.

Monday, Monday was known for its salad bar. Ingrid and Oscar had gone there religiously in the early days of their relationship—the "salad days," now that she thought about it—when more than one or two things had seemed possible. The salad bar had everything you could think of and everything you couldn't: subzero iceberg and waxy cucumbers and electric purple onions. Banana chips, imitation crab, aspic, chowchow. It was a lesson in both bliss and absurdity.

Ingrid stood in the wide entrance of Monday, Monday and watched the customers fret over the salad bar. It was demanding. It belittled. Ingrid guessed ten percent of its items were unrecognizable, and these items left patrons feeling ignorant. One time, Oscar had pointed to jicama, and she'd said "jicama," and he'd asked her to spell it, and he'd refused to believe it began with a *j*. Ingrid had seethed then, and she seethed now.

That was when Ingrid saw him—Oscar—right there in Monday, Monday. His familiar bald spot, his worn Cincinnati Reds jacket with its giant pinched *C*. It was the back of him, she was sure of it, moving slowly down the salad bar. Unless, Ingrid squinted, it was not. She recognized the shoes, but not the patience. The posture struck a chord, but not the way the man pointed, kindly, to the woman beside him. The man, who Ingrid felt certain she both did and did not know, had two plates on his tray. He appeared to be naming the items on the salad bar, reaching for them with the tongs and making two salads while the woman beside him watched. The man pointed and plated, pointed and plated while the woman nodded and shrugged, nodded and shrugged. The woman was short. Shorter than most. *Happy,* thought Ingrid. *Sleepy, Dopey, Bashful, Mindy.* Ingrid's stomach stirred again, as it had on the mattress with Malcolm. She thought of all the times she and Oscar had gone through the motions. When had the choices dwindled to two—stay or go—for her and Oscar? When had it all gone wrong? Miscarriage three or six? Five or seven? The money they'd spent on unborn children had turned Ingrid's brown hair gray, Oscar's blue eyes gray.

Maybe-Oscar and Maybe-Mindy reached the end of the salad bar. He carried the tray, and she carried herself like someone who liked having her tray carried. Ingrid thought briefly of the Canadian in college, of how he'd unfastened her bra one-handed. Of how he'd taken her bottom lip into his mouth and made her feel like anything was possible. It was as if he'd known what the options were in life and he'd reported them back to her. Babies, marriage, divorce. Giraffes and lions and wildebeest. Macaroni and cheese, macaroni without. Jicama.

Maybe later, Ingrid would go back to the mattress store. Maybe she would get back on the memory foam and tell Malcolm about the lost babies. How she'd named them Ward, Anna, Theo, and Ike. Jennifer, Michael, and Poppy. Maybe she'd tell him how the remains of one of the babies had been substantial enough to fish from the toilet and bury in a potted ficus at home. How she still had the ficus. How the ficus had been the one thing she'd saved from the burning bedroom. Or maybe Ingrid would go back to Queen B. and buy the yellow overalls. Maybe she'd put them on, still with their tags, and stand outside of Monday, Monday. *Over here!* the fluorescent pants would say without her having to. *See me? Look at me! Here I am.* Maybe, if the man turned around, and she saw that it was Oscar, she'd break. Maybe she'd run to him, climb him, beg him, beat him.

Ingrid watched the man and woman choose a table. The whole time, it was only their backs. She never saw their faces. But she did see their bed. It was a waterbed and it was on fire. A weak flame spread across the plastic, slow and sad, until, at last, the bed gaped open and the water gushed onto the floor, signaling the start of a long and difficult labor.

The Yardstick

After Isaac's father left Isaac and his mother for a flight attendant named Deidra, Isaac and his mother went back to the town his mother was originally from, a place as nondescript and predictable as she was. For two plane tickets and a deposit on a rental duplex, Isaac's mother sold her used Plymouth and the small gold watch her grandmother had given her when she'd graduated from high school. She cried in the pawnshop as she slid the watch across the glass case, showing, it seemed to Isaac, more sorrow for the watch's predicament than her own son's. While the broker counted out twelve fresh twenties, Isaac went and stood by a gumball machine, wounded. For the first time, he allowed himself to see his mother as his father had, a villain instead of a victim, and in doing so, Isaac felt an unexpected but immediate relief, like a yawn or a sneeze. Out in the pawnshop's parking lot, when the transaction was complete, Isaac did not take his mother's outstretched hand. Instead, he put his fists into the pockets of his tweed car coat and looked up at the sky. He imagined his father and Deidra above clouds, laughing and as close to heaven as two alive people could get.

When Isaac and his mother arrived in Missouri, Isaac decided he would no longer speak. His grandfather picked him and his mother up at the airport and drove them to a diner where he bought them both omelets and announced that the meal and the car ride were the last favors he'd be doing for them now that they'd gotten themselves into their predicament. To punish his grandfather for considering him an accomplice, Isaac refused to eat his eggs. He kept his vow of silence when they arrived at the little duplex in the spartan neighborhood, even when the landlady—who lived on the left side of the house—came out smiling and waving and smelling of cocoa butter to show Isaac and his mother the right side.

"Isaac, can't you say hello?" his mother said, squeezing his upper arm in a way that felt like further betrayal. "I don't think he's going to talk," she explained weakly as they stood in the cold front yard. "He's had a tough time."

"Haven't we all," the lady said cheerfully. "Well, I'm Ms. Glisson and I'm glad you're here. I'm never more than a knock away." Isaac saw that the lady's auburn hair was piled on her head like a towel and fastened with a thousand black hairpins, shiny ants in a nest of red earth. "I just had the carpets shampooed for you and the grout cleaned as best grout can be cleaned. And tonight I'd like you to come over for dinner and a craft project. I've made moussaka."

Isaac didn't know what moussaka was and he knew his mother didn't either, but he knew she'd say yes, both to start things off right and for a free meal.

"Thank you," his mother said more weakly than before. "We won't say no to that."

Inside the plain duplex, Isaac and his mother set down their four suitcases. Two mattresses had been delivered, both twins, and they were propped against the living room wall like a pair of teepees. There was a cardboard box of dishes that had been sent from their former life, as well as a card table and two folding chairs that Ms. Glisson had unfolded. On the table was a bowl of apples with a handwritten note.

I got you apples instead of bananas! it said. *Because bananas, like men, never stay good for long!* Then there was a smiley face drawn in ballpoint, with one eye open and one eye closed, like it was winking. It was signed with a big and dramatic *MS. G!*

Isaac's mother crumpled up the note and threw it into a corner of the room. "We don't even have a trash can," she said. "I've had to go and sell a family heirloom for things like trash cans, and what do you think he's doing right now?" Isaac's mother turned and looked at her son as if he knew the answer. "Her. That's what he's doing. Her, her, her." Then she went and locked herself into the bathroom and turned on the tub.

Isaac could hear his mother crying as he stood in the living room in his car coat. *I even had it engraved!* he heard his mother say. Isaac wasn't sure what to do, but eventually he ate one apple and then another. When he was done, he went outside and threw the cores into the front shrubs, then he came back in and retrieved Ms. Glisson's crumpled note. He smoothed it with his hands and refolded it with care and put it into his pocket. When his mother finally appeared wearing the red turtleneck she'd worn to the divorce proceedings, he noticed it matched her eyes.

"Shall we?" his mother sighed. Isaac gave a loose shrug.

Ms. Glisson's door was hung with a tinsel shamrock and she opened the door wide before Isaac and his mother could even knock. "*Buenas noches!*" she exclaimed. "*Benvenuto!*"

Isaac and his mother stepped inside and stopped on the miniscule square of parquet flooring. The left side of duplex was nothing like the right side. Ms. Glisson's side smelled of lamb and cinnamon. The walls were papered in a metallic trellis design. There was a birdcage filled with ferns, a couch the color of wine, a coffee table made of stained glass and piled with craft supplies. The carpet was as white and deep as a February snow.

"Here," Ms. Glisson said. "I hope you don't mind." She handed Isaac and his mother each a pair of paper sandals. "I learned this trick in Japan," she said. "The Japanese. They're light years ahead of us. At least in this regard," she motioned to her sock feet. "Feet and photography."

Isaac took off his sneakers and put on the paper shoes. As he walked, his socks slid on the paper and the paper slid on the carpet. He knew it was like ice skating even though he'd never been ice skating.

"I figure we'll eat first, craft second," Ms. Glisson said, and Isaac and his mother did as they were told. They each took a large yellow plate when it was handed to them, and they each let Ms. Glisson pile the plate with moussaka and salad. "Do you like Catalina?" Ms. Glisson asked. "I don't mean the island owned by the chewing gum people, I mean the salad dressing." She picked up a big plastic bottle and shook it as proof. "It's like French but more agreeable." Isaac gave another flimsy raise of his shoulders, and Ms. Glisson poured the dressing over a mound of iceberg and shredded carrots. "Really. They should just call it British."

Isaac and his mother took their loaded plates and sat at the dining table which was in the same room as the wine-colored sofa and the kitchen. "These duplexes aren't big," Ms. Glisson said. "But I've had big—*very* big, actually—and it's overrated." She winked at Isaac's mother. "If you get my drift."

Isaac watched his mother turn pink. He looked back and forth between the two women and then down at his plate. "Take men for what they're good for, I say. Their seed and wallet. Nothing more, nothing less."

Ms. Glisson reached for a crystal bottle with a stopper that looked like a giant emerald. She poured herself a glass of something the color of syrup and did the same for Isaac's mother. "I got my son Johnny and five thousand from my first marriage, and Rhapsody—my daughter, not the emotional state—and one hundred thousand from the second." Ms. Glisson took a long sip and refilled her glass. "It doesn't look like you made off with much. But you've got this young fellow here and maybe he'll grow up to be one of the good ones. Or gay ones." Ms. Glisson smiled at Isaac with encouragement. "Plus. I'll go easy on the rent until summer. No sense in a child starting school this late in the year. And no sense in you running around ragged looking for work until it's warm."

Isaac looked at his mother. She was good and pink now, but her eyes were no longer red. She drank what was in her glass and Ms. Glisson refilled it, and then they all pushed their dishes away with gusto before gathering around the coffee table.

"We're going to make yardstick holders," Ms. Glisson announced. She knelt as easily as a child and clapped her hands together once. Her dress dipped low to show her cleavage. Between her breasts, Isaac could see some sort of pendant sleeping. "I even bought you a yardstick to put in the yardstick holder, because I figured you might need one." Ms. Glisson spread out burlap in front of Isaac and burlap in front of herself. "Isaac and I will do the work, Cora. You just sit and drink."

Isaac had never known his mother to have more than a single cold beer at a cookout, but Ms. Glisson kept refilling her glass and his mother didn't refuse. Ms. Glisson showed Isaac what to do by pointing to her work and then pointing at his supplies.

"Here's the truth, Cora," Ms. Glisson said. "Women live in a constant state of shock. We can't believe men are as heartless as they are, but they are, and we spend the first thirty years of our lives just not believing it's possible." Isaac saw he was to cut a plum from purple felt and an orange from orange felt and an apple from red felt. He worked a pair of shears larger than he was normally allowed to operate around the thick felt and produced three lopsided circles. "When we finally admit that men are incapable of love, it's a big relief." Ms. Glisson showed Isaac where to squeeze three generous squeezes of glue. "Well, grief, then relief. You have to give yourself some time to cry about it, I suppose, but don't get stuck there. At some point, you've got to get off the couch and take the garbage to the curb."

Ms. Glisson folded Isaac's strip of burlap in half. The fruit he'd cut out dotted one side like a crude and narrow stoplight. "In the craft world, we call this sort of thing a cozy," she said. "It's like a sleeping bag. I've made them for toasters, coffeepots, blenders. Speaking of sleeping bags," Ms. Glisson said, "I have two for you and your mother to use until we get you both some decent bed linens. What sort of linens do you like, Cora? Cotton? Flannel? Polyester?" Isaac looked over to see that his mother had fallen asleep.

"That's what I was hoping for," Ms. Glisson smiled. "Leave your burlap for me to sew, and head on home, Isaac. I'll walk your mother over and then come back with the sleeping bags. Your mother will likely feel poorly in the morning," Ms. Glisson said. "So play quietly until she wakes up. At some point tomorrow, I'll bring your yardstick holder over. You can hang it on the wall of your new house and your mother can take the yardstick out once a month to see how tall you're getting."

Ms. Glisson was right. The next morning, Isaac's mother felt terrible. She spent a good deal of time in the bathroom coughing and crying before coming back out to the living room and curling up on her twin mattress.

"That woman," she moaned. "She should know better than to do that to someone so vulnerable."

But then, at ten, Ms. Glisson was at their door with the finished yardstick holder and two shopping bags filled with new towels and bed linens. "I also have breakfast for you," she beamed. "I'll be right back."

Before Isaac's mother could refuse, Ms. Glisson was returning from across the way with a big bamboo tray of coffee and bread. "These are French," she said, breaking open a roll and handing it to Isaac. "When I went to Paris on my second ex's dime, I discovered real bread and real romance." She handed Isaac's mother a cup of coffee. "Mind you, I didn't say love, I said romance. I'm talking about the loins, not loneliness. Don't bring your heart into the bedroom, Cora, and you'll have a good go at things."

Ms. Glisson went to her purse and brought out a bottle of aspirin. She shook out two and handed them to Isaac's mother.

Then she clapped her hands together as she had the night before. "Now let's hang the yardstick holder, Isaac. You pick the place."

Isaac crammed what was left of the roll into his mouth. He walked around the small duplex and finally chose a narrow strip of kitchen wall for his narrow strip of burlap. Before she hammered a nail, Ms. Glisson took the yardstick and measured Isaac's height. She took a pencil out from behind her ear and drew a line and then wrote the date.

"How old are you, Isaac? Nine?"

"Seven," Isaac said. "And a half."

"Well, you better measure yourself twice a month then. Seven is a busy year." Ms. Glisson hammered a small nail into the wall and hung the holder right where Isaac had asked. "Measure yourself until you're a man, and then there's no point in measuring at all."

For the rest of that first month, Ms. Glisson came over at least twice a day. She brought metal bed frames from the Goodwill and an old dresser that she helped Isaac's mother paint purple. She loaned them four of her big yellow plates and four yellow mugs and four yellow bowls. She brought them beach chairs to use in their living room until they could afford a couch. One afternoon, she wheeled in a cart full of African violets. One weekend, she got them both library cards. And, every few days, she went and made too much soup for herself and had to bring them several quarts to eat or freeze. Most importantly, it seemed to Isaac that Ms. Glisson knew just what to do to keep his mother from crying.

"Now, now," she'd say, when Isaac's mother would start to look bereft. "That's not how we handle liberation, Cora. Do we need to do a craft? Is a craft in order, Isaac?"

To which Isaac would nod, more for his own sake than his mother's, and Ms. Glisson would go back to her apartment to retrieve the supplies that struck her fancy, as well as the crystal bottle with the emerald stopper. Isaac's mother would drink—sometimes until sleep—while Isaac and Ms. Glisson made whatever she decided they should make.

At first, the crafts were benign, boring even—birdhouses and toothbrush holders and oven mitts. But as Isaac settled in, and Isaac's mother settled down, Ms. Glisson showed up with coins and candles, hunks of rocks and bowls of salt, as well as a second crystal bottle with an emerald stopper. While Isaac's mother sipped and sniffed, Ms. Glisson would sing songs in a language Isaac didn't know. She'd mark their foreheads with oil and ashes. She'd lay out cards in a willy-nilly pattern and ask Isaac to turn them over. One night, he turned over a card with a picture of a man who had a rope around his neck.

"Oh, me. It's the Hanged Man," Ms. Glisson sighed. "No surprise there, Isaac. It's your father. But also *my* father. It's *all* the fathers. The universe is telling us to steer clear of men."

Isaac looked to his mother to see what she thought of this. He expected her to frown, to maybe even ask Ms. Glisson to leave. But instead she smiled slow and sleepy from her low-slung beach chair and whispered: "Fuck fathers. Fuck them all."

Isaac's breath escaped him. Ms. Glisson clapped her hands together in delight. In the glow of the candles, while Isaac pressed his stomach, Ms. Glisson's eyes went bright at some new idea, and she got up from her place on the floor. Her pendant swung out from between her breasts as she rose, out into the night like a pendulum counting the seconds, and then back into the dark valley by her heart. "I need to help your mother to bed, Isaac. You stay here and let me get her to where she needs to be."

Ms. Glisson pulled Isaac's mother up from her chair. The two of them walked slow and unsteady into the second tiny bedroom and closed the door. Isaac sat in the living room as he had on that first day and listened for his mother's muffled emotional state. He heard her laugh. He heard her gasp. He heard her call out for a god she'd recently told Isaac she no longer believed in. And, after some time, after the candles had burned themselves out, Ms. Glisson reappeared in the blue glow of moonlight to gather her things. Isaac could not see her face, but the hair that she normally wore up on her head like a towel had been let down and her voice was one Isaac had never heard before, stern and unflinching.

"Your mother isn't feeling well, Isaac," she said. "I've gotten her to bed and I think you should leave her alone until the sun is nice and high."

When Ms. Glisson was gone with her two empty bottles and bag of supplies, Isaac, defiant, went into his mother's bedroom to see for himself what sort of state she was in. He found her face down and sprawled like a star, snoring quietly. Her back was bare and the sheet was caught around her waist. Isaac remembered when he'd been allowed to come into his parents' bedroom in the night. When he'd been allowed—invited, even—to sleep between the two of them, hot and still and safe. Isaac reached out to touch his mother's back, but decided against it, and when he turned to leave her as he'd found her, his bare foot landed on something cold and round—a coin or a circle of spilled water. But when he reached down to see, it was the pendant—Ms. Glisson's—rogue and unchained.

Isaac took it with him into his bedroom and turned on his

overhead light. The pendant was silver and worn, engraved with two overlapping circles, and when Isaac put his fingernail along its edge, the pendant became a locket and opened to reveal a single curl of black hair. Isaac's breath escaped him for the second time that night. He closed the locket at once, only to open it again and close it again. He did this four or five times, his heart quickening with each repetition, until he eventually convinced himself—was wholly certain—that the hair inside was his own.

Isaac lay on his mattress for a long time, trying to think of where he could hide the necklace in the barren apartment. There was no place he could think of that it wouldn't be found. Finally, before dawn turned the black sky blue, Isaac went to the refrigerator. He opened one of Ms. Glisson's quarts of soup and he dropped the pendant into it. Then he got one of the folding chairs and he brought it to the kitchen so he could reach the freezer, and he put the quart of soup behind all the other quarts, in the freezer's coldest, farthest part. When he was done, Isaac went to bed. He couldn't say if he slept or not.

The next day, Ms. Glisson came to visit earlier than usual. She started off sly and sweet about the necklace, but once the right side of the duplex had been turned inside out and the left side of the duplex had been turned upside down, and still no pendant had been found, Ms. Glisson turned surly. "I can't do a thing without it," she said. "It's sentimental and important and I haven't taken it off since the day I received it. This will *not* do."

"Is it from your children?" Isaac's mother asked. "The man in France?"

"No and no!" Ms. Glisson snapped. "It's none of your business unless it *is* your business and you or your boy has put it somewhere secret." Ms. Glisson glared at Isaac as she said this, and to Isaac's delight, his mother came close to glaring at Ms. Glisson.

"I know Isaac and I have accepted nearly everything you've graciously given us," Isaac's mother said. "But we aren't crooks. We aren't opportunists."

Ms. Glisson crossed her arms and tapped her foot on the small parquet entry. "Is that so?" she said. "Do you remember anything of last night?" Isaac looked at his mother and his mother looked at the floor. "There you go," Ms. Glisson said. "There you have it."

Ms. Glisson didn't come by the whole next week. Isaac's mother began to worry about what she'd do for food and what she'd do for rent and Isaac began to worry about the soup. He feared that now they would go through it sooner rather than later and his mother would find the pendant in the slush of some thawed chowder and the bond that was once again growing between them would break for a second time.

"Maybe I should go to school," Isaac said. "Then you can get a job."

But that afternoon, on their doorstep, Isaac's mother found a fresh crystal bottle with an emerald stopper, and she came inside and drank until she was happy and then until she was sad.

"Maybe we should call Grandpa," Isaac suggested. "Maybe I should write Dad."

But those ideas were the worst ideas that anyone could have and Isaac's mother told him so. "Those are the worst ideas anyone could have." She staggered to the front door and opened it. The spring night came in like a way out, until Isaac's mother set the empty bottle on the welcome mat and shut the door. "Didn't you hear anything the landlady said?" Isaac's mother steadied herself with one hand on the folding table. "We have to take the garbage to the curb."

Every morning, Isaac and his mother thawed a quart of soup, and every afternoon there was a new bottle on the doorstep, and every night his mother drank the entire thing. When only two quarts of soup remained in the freezer, Isaac let his mother thaw the next to last one, and when she went to bed, he thawed the final one in a sink filled with hot water. At the bottom of the chowder, he fished out the pendant. Then he rinsed it and shined it, and with much trepidation opened it. The hair inside had been ruined by the soup. Before it had frozen, or while it had thawed, the broth had seeped into the pendant's small crack and made the lock of black hair into an oily mess. So, Isaac did what needed to be done. He rinsed the old hair down the drain and dried the locket's insides and then went into the bathroom and used his mother's nail scissors to cut a new lock—a twin to the one he'd ruined—and he tucked it inside. When the pendant looked as it had the night he'd found it, he set it on the floor of his mother's bedroom, right by her bed, so she could be the one to find it.

Ms. Glisson took the pendant from Isaac's mother with skepticism. She squinted at its front and back. She held it to her nose. At last, she turned from Isaac and his mother and Isaac could hear her click the pendant open and shut. She stood with her back to them for quite some time. Then she turned to face them, expressionless, and asked, "Why now and not sooner?"

Isaac's mother put both of her hands on Isaac's shoulders and shrugged innocently. "Because now is when I found it," she said. "I got out of bed this morning and there it was. On the floor. I nearly stepped on it."

Ms. Glisson smiled in a way that Isaac recognized as forced and false, but his mother did not. When his mother went to make everyone tea, Ms. Glisson got down on Isaac's level. She put the pendant back on its chain and let it slide down to its home between her breasts. She gave it a pat and then gazed up at Isaac, in what appeared to be approval. "A man," she said plainly. "That's what we have here."

Soon after that, Isaac's mother brought out the tea and the tea was had by all three, and by the end of the day things were as they once had been with Ms. Glisson. There was not just soup but also cookies and two crystal bottles with emerald stoppers. There were stories of France and stories of Japan and a promise to bring over a set of skillets and a raincoat Ms. Glisson had long outgrown. That night no one was a villain or a victim.

When summer came around, full and lush and green, and Isaac started feeling tall, it occurred to him that he hadn't been measured in a while, but when he went to get the yardstick, he found that it, and its holder, were gone. The nail was gone, too. Even the hole the nail had made was nowhere to be found. Isaac's previous heights and the dates, the ones that had been recorded in pencil, had vanished. Isaac stared for some time at the empty narrow strip of kitchen wall, looking for a fleck of eraser, or a speck of paint that filled the hole, but he couldn't find anything of the sort. At first, he was perplexed, but later, as the sun warmed his new yard and new life, he didn't think much about it, not really at all. He went on doing what he did. He let Ms. Glisson and his mother do what they did down the hall, and he imagined what his father and Deidra might be doing and he let them do that, too. It wasn't until the fall, when Isaac went to school and his mother got a job and they were finally able to buy a couch, that Isaac really thought about the yardstick. One night, he dropped something behind the sofa, and when he realized that the yardstick would have been the perfect thing to reach that which was just beyond reach, only then did he feel its absence. Only then, on his knees, looking into a dark space, did he see what he'd never get back.

Beans

On her *sixtieth* birthday, Leslie received a padded manila envelope in the mail from a national senior citizens association. Inside was a mass-produced greeting card that said *LOOK HOW YOU'VE GROWN!* along with a packet of heirloom seeds. The seeds were labeled in all caps—*TANGENT BEANS*—and sported a subtitle of miniscule, italicized print that read: *garden for a healthy mind.* Leslie, who had been incrementally and secretly reducing her medicinal intake in the hopes of once again thinking thoughts and feeling feelings, was instantly offended. This was clearly the work of her husband Dale and her neurologist-slash-Dale's golfing buddy, Dr. Neil Nesbitt. Dale and Neil had been in manipulative cahoots since their fraternity days, beginning with the hazing of hapless undergrads and culminating in the intellectual pruning of inquisitive Leslie.

"My wife suffers from overthought" was how Dale had put it

to Dr. Nesbitt, seven years prior, when his extracurricular activities had gone public.

To which Dr. Nesbitt, while needlessly prodding Leslie's neck glands and smiling the way farmers smile at November turkeys, had said, "I have just the thing."

The thing was thrice daily capsules the size of asparagus tips and once weekly electrodes, a combo that rendered Leslie blank and bland and . . . and . . . what was the word? At the six-week follow-up, Leslie was shown a "before" image of her brain activity next to an "after" image. One was fire, one ice. Vesuvius and Antarctica. Jambalaya, mashed potatoes.

"So, tell me," Dr. Nesbitt beamed. "How do you feel?"

Next to Dale in the examination room, in a chair that felt neither hard nor soft nor just right, Leslie was incapable of producing the necessary vocabulary. Instead, her torpid mind coughed up a flickering vision, a clot of symbolic phlegm. It was a wan picture of the local IGA where she regularly forgot what she had gone in for. She saw the grocery store's back alley, its cod-colored cinder blocks, a forgotten cabbage on its loading dock. The cabbage had one loose leaf that flapped in the wind like a celery-colored comb-over. It was waving, weakly, at Leslie. Dr. Nesbitt and Dale waited, stared. Leslie opened her mouth to say what it was that she saw, but only one word came out. "Vegetable."

Dr. Nesbitt nodded at Dale. Dale nodded at Dr. Nesbitt. Leslie felt herself nodding, nodding, nodding off.

Again, that was seven years ago, and Leslie recalled all of it as she considered the generic birthday card and shook the packet of beans. They sounded like horse pills. Trachea busters. Leslie knew the sensation all too well. A fist in a sock. Dr. Nesbitt had eventually upped her daily intake to eight monstrous capsules, her weekly electrodes to M, T, W, R. That was how he'd put it. "Zap you on M, T, W, R, Leslie!" But on her fifty-ninth birthday, at the urging of Franklin, the electrode nurse who "loved to feel," Leslie had given herself the gift of weaning. It had taken almost nine months for her to go from eight capsules to four, but in doing so, she'd halved her oblivion.

It wasn't easy. There were side effects that rivaled vision quests. Leslie had seen spots. Static, tie-dyed swirls behind her eye sockets. Fireworks, Shasta daisies, shivering cells merging and dividing. Some mornings, she'd felt like she was walking the circumference of a black volcanic mouth. Sometimes the devil appeared behind her in the bathroom mirror. He had the face of her high school chemistry teacher and cloven goat feet he placed on her shoulders. He said things like "I know where Dale keeps the ammo!" and "Look at you, you filthy slut." But Leslie had kept going. The fear and sweats were at least fear and sweats. They weren't blahs and mehs or huhs and whatevers. Leslie had persevered, both in the face of terror and in search of it. The way she saw it, horror bested ho-hum, so three times a day, she'd taken the box cutter and shaved down each pill. She had a little help from vodka, a little from a crucifix, and a lot from Franklin who agreed to attach the electrodes to her biceps instead of her temples in exchange for off-duty hand jobs. "You'll thank me for this," he said. Which Leslie went on and did, because even at four pills a day, she had started to remember the word for gratitude.

Leslie shook the beans. Leslie read the card again. Now it was her big 6-0. See how much she'd grown? What was she going to gift herself now? Gardening? She looked in the foyer mirror.

"My oh my," the devil whistled. "Someone's gotten too big for her britches."

Leslie brushed the cloven hooves from her shoulders as easily as dandruff. She opened the tangent beans and shook two into her palm. They were pear green and the size of earplugs. She placed them on her tongue and swallowed them whole. They settled near the hollow of her throat, bullets in a gun. Leslie knew it was finally time. She went into the bedroom and put on the white sack dress that Dale hated. She packed a suitcase with underwear and sweaters, the bean seeds, the birthday card, a pen, a notebook. She went back to the foyer and stood and stared into the den, at the back of Dale's head.

"I'm leaving," she said.

Dale didn't look away from whatever it was he'd been looking at for thirty-five years: the NASDAQ, cubes falling from an electronic sky and sliding into geometric order, men in plaid pants with white balls and metal sticks traversing green fields. "Ehn," he grunted.

Leslie closed the door behind her before Dale could ask her to pick up milk on her way back, even though she was neither going to the store nor coming back. She was going to the forest, about an hour away, to the land and building she'd bought with money she'd earned over the past year by donating plasma and blood and stool. Turned out her stool had been valuable. It wasn't much of a building. It was just one of those sheds for sale in the parking lot of Home Depot, painted maroon to resemble a tiny barn and complete with buttermilk trim and Xs on the doors. But it was hers. A week earlier, she'd hired someone named Floyd to trailer it out to the half acre on the cliff, hook her up a composting toilet and a generator. A little tank of water and a little tank of propane. A barrel for trash burning.

"Not much of a place for a woman your age," Floyd said when he was done.

Leslie chopped off Floyd's head with a look. She'd been completely off any pills for two days by then, and the facts were starting to come out. "At my age, I'm not much of a woman." After that, Floyd shut up, and Leslie smiled. A real smile for the first time in quite some time.

For the first week in the woods, Leslie wrapped the tangent beans in wet paper towels and left them in the sun. Then she took a spiral notebook and filled it with all the wrongs ever done to her. Without any medication, the wrongs were the first things Leslie's brain threw off, and she surprised herself by writing nine pages about a single incident that had occurred at the Dairy Barn when she was four. She had licked an entire scoop of grape sherbet right off the top of her sugar cone and onto the orange tile, and her stepfather had lost his mind. "Jesus Christ!" he'd shouted. It was 1957, South Carolina, and "fiddlesticks" was still borderline obscene. Visibly, the other patrons in the ice cream shop took the outburst hard. The scoop was quite large in Leslie's memory, a purple softball-sized mound that her stepfather bent down and retrieved bare-handed, then threw at the silver swinging door of the trash receptacle, where it landed with an audible splat. Everyone present took note of this for a few silent seconds, before her stepfather yanked Leslie's left arm up and nearly out of its socket and paraded her from the store.

Leslie listed on a blank page in her notebook who she'd felt most sorry for that day. Number one: the patrons who had had to see such a scene. Number two: the employee who'd scooped the ice cream and neglected to press it firmly into the sugar cone; he probably blamed himself. Number three: whoever had to come and clean the orange tile floor and the trash can's door. Perhaps the same employee? A tragic possibility. Number four: her step-father. How wretched to be so wretched. Leslie was not religious, but she did believe in hell because, above all else, she believed in justice. Leslie felt certain her stepfather, who had died from a perforated ulcer when she was twelve, was in hell. Not just for the ice cream incident, but for a portfolio of similar occurrences that, when presented together, made an airtight case for eternal damnation. Number five: Jesus Christ. Again, not religious, but Jesus was a historical figure known for doing some pretty nice things and thus undeserving of such ill verbal memorializing. Number six: herself.

To be sure, there were other things in the notebook—Dale's affairs (at least the three she knew of), Dale making her get her head checked repeatedly, Dale making her take the pills, Dale and the doctor teaming up on her the way men do with opinionated women—but it was the ice cream entry that proved most therapeutic, and once the spiral notebook was filled with all notable slights, Leslie took it to the trash barrel and set it on fire. She let the notebook burn until the spiral was a red-hot coil, a hungry tendril, and in that incendiary time, Leslie stood over the barrel rubbing her hands together, even though it was June and her hands were not particularly cold. Afterward, she went and looked at the beans. They had sprouted fine, anemic hairs and looked like the tiny decapitated heads of old white men. Namely, husbands and doctors and men who trailered sheds to and from the woods and commented on the age of women.

*

The second week, Leslie planted the tangent beans. Though there was no real excavated land for a proper garden, there was sunshine here and there around her little red building, and Leslie went to and fro in the surrounding grass and leaves and underbrush, around the bases of trees, and poked the hairy beans into the earth. Beside each poke, she slid a piece of dried willow into the ground, and onto each branch of dried willow, she tied a piece of string. When she was finished poking and sliding and tying, Leslie gathered all the strings and ran them back to her house and tied them all to a big metal eye hook near the roof. Soon enough, her house would be covered in vines and beans and she could sit under the vines and beans, and eat the beans raw and with her hands, in the shade of what she herself had made, no matter what it did to her digestively.

By the third week, there was not much else to do in the woods with the tangent beans now in the ground, and Leslie found herself sitting in her camp chair most of the time, staring out at the wooded hills and thinking. Her thoughts were now coming back to life with vigor and vengeance, all over the place, branching and winding this way and that, but on that third week her mind found something of a focused path and she mostly thought about sex. Not about having it or missing it, just the various acts thereof, and how they, when considered as a whole, were truly abhorrent. Leslie counted eleven ways: penis in vagina, penis in mouth, penis in hand, penis in ass crack, penis in ass, penis between two breasts. Then there were two vaginas smashed together, vagina on face, finger(s) on vagina, finger(s) in vagina, finger(s) in ass. Leslie sat in her camp chair and stared out over the Daniel Boone National Forest. Technically, she supposed it was not really two vaginas smashed together, a vagina on a face, or finger(s) on a vagina. Technically, she guessed these specific scenarios actually involved vulvas, so she changed the terminology in her head and went through the positions a second time, trying to be more scientifically precise. While she did this, she also wondered if the plural of "vulva" was actually "vulvas" or "vulvae." Or perhaps it was a word, like "fish" or "deer," where the singular was also the plural. One vulva, two vulva. One deer, five fish.

The pills had kept Leslie from thinking about anything interesting for decades, and without them, her brain ignited. *Watch this,* it seemed to shout. After the positions and the possibilities came the friction. Leslie thought of all the frantic rubbing that had occurred since the dawn of humanity—the chafing, the desperation—and it reminded Leslie of those two-person saws that were used by lumberjacks to take down sequoias. In her mind, she heard the saw go back and forth until it took down an entire rainforest. She saw mounds and mounds—mountain ranges, really—of fresh, orange sawdust. Leslie thought of the millions of years of repetitive sex. She saw a world deforested. She was physically ill. Leslie went to the trash barrel and vomited her disgust onto the deteriorating black spiral.

Back in her camp chair, Leslie looked at the trees and asked herself: *What is humanity's path?* She asked herself: *What is its opposite?* Leslie didn't know, but whatever the opposite was, she made a promise to do just that. She looked out at the tangent beans and saw that they were slowly coming in green now. Bright chartreuse spirals could be seen here and there in the grass, coiled and perfect as prom hair, ready for the dance.

Every two weeks, Floyd came by with gasoline and propane and water and whatever else Leslie had asked him to bring from the last visit. That was the thing: when Leslie thought of something she wanted—a new pencil, dried cherries, salt—she had to wait and place her order the next time Floyd came around. So, if she thought of something right after he left, it was nearly a month before she got it. She could have probably used a pistol. Sunglasses. Cornmeal. A book of crosswords. A pet canary with clipped wings. There wasn't much yellow out here.

"Don't you think someone is missing you?" Floyd asked on his third resupply. Floyd was the only person who knew where she was. He didn't know who she was, which was a relief, but still, Leslie wished she'd hired a woman to get her hauled out and settled in the first place.

"Missing me personally?" Leslie asked. "Or my services?" Floyd stood and looked at her like he didn't know the difference, because he didn't. "I am confident," Leslie said, "that someone misses my orifices and chicken chili. But me?" She almost said her full name aloud but instead stopped short and yanked the first bean of the season from a willow branch at her calf. She split the bean open in her palm and tossed the pale pearls within it into her mouth like medicine. "You don't miss what you don't know."

Floyd gave her a long, hard look when he drove away. It was a look that said he might have to say something to someone about her whereabouts. Talking like she had had likely made Floyd feel stupid, which he was, and Leslie knew that a man made to feel stupid by a woman would go to no end to put that woman in danger, or at least spoil her fun. Leslie promptly devised an escape plan before Floyd could return with either the supplies she had requested or the sheriff she had not. She started with water. She hauled every drop of water she had, save for one thermos, out in a coffee cup to each tangent bean plant, and gave each plant four cups to drink. Then she went to her composting toilet and tore the wood seat from its top and, dipping down and using the same coffee cup she had for the water, she filled the cup and went back out and gave every tangent bean plant two cups of waste. It was her waste, just like it had been her plasma and her blood and her stool and her bone marrow, and this made Leslie feel good, as if she were dismantling herself for something bigger and better.

When the tangent beans were watered and fed, Leslie sat in her camp chair, facing away from the plants and tried to work out, once again, the idea of a path and its opposite. But one thought wrapped around another and made Leslie tired. She closed her eyes and fell asleep. She dreamed briefly of sex, was disgusted, announced in her dream she was neither heterosexual nor homosexual but a Leslian. She dreamed she pulled a string through her mind to give her thoughts something to follow. She screwed an eye hook into her forehead, between her eyes, and tethered the string there and waited for her thoughts to get in line. When she woke late morning, she could hear the birds, she could hear the wind in the trees. But she could hear something fainter still that sounded like the opposite of sawing, like the opposite of back and forth. Without opening her eyes, Leslie knew it was the tangent beans, growing. They had finally out-grown the willow branches and were now winding around the strings. It was not unlike a symphony. Leslie thought of what she'd said to Floyd—*you don't miss what you don't know*—and realized she was wrong. She'd never even wondered what beans growing might sound like, but as she sat there listening to the beans do just that, Leslie realized she'd been missing it her entire life.

Thanks to the water and waste, by afternoon, the sprouts had grown into stalks as thick as Leslie's ankles. The plants uprooted the willow branches, they sagged the strings tied to the eye hook, the eye hook bulged from the wood composite of the red shed, and Leslie, delighted, could not contain herself. She climbed up on the roof as easily as a goat. She tied a clothesline through the eye hook and then looped the clothesline over the lowest branch of a tulip poplar and then back around through the eye hook. The sound of the growing beans grew louder than the birds, louder than the wind through the trees. If Floyd returned, which Leslie felt certain he would, there was no way she'd hear the sound of his truck, so she decided to sit on the peak of the shed for lookout—humming within, unfurling along with the beans—in her white dress, which was no longer white, with one leg draped over each side of the roof, like she was straddling the spine of a book. The spiral of a notebook.

In an hour's time, the beanstalks had wrapped around Leslie's entire body, from her ankles to armpits. In two hours, she was nothing more than a woman in a green fist, being carried up, by no will of her own, to a heaven she did not believe in. In three hours, the beanstalk had outgrown the tulip poplar by so much, Leslie's shed resembled a red notebook, the trash barrel a scoop of melting purple. By dinner, Leslie had no desire to eat, because she herself was being eaten, was she not? Finally, when Floyd's truck arrived at dusk, as Leslie had suspected it might, Leslie could hardly make out that there were two men with him. Three men in total. Three white beans moving here and there, around Floyd's black truck like three dots that had escaped a domino. *Floyd, Dale, Dr. Neil Nesbitt,* Leslie thought.

Leslie looked up to where she was heading and back to where she had been. The word "deviate" came to mind. But the word Leslie said aloud was "Deviant!" She was closer now to the stars than she was to her roots. And if someone wanted her down now, they'd have their work cut out for them. No telling how many saws it would take. How many hands and bodies, how much time and friction. Leslie didn't think there were enough of those things on earth to bring her back. From what she guessed, the whole world could go back and forth, back and forth, forever and ever, and by the time they were even close to bringing her down, she would have already grown up.

Threesome

Mrs. Skelton never cooks. She pours cereal for dinner and sits at the end of the table with her saccharine soda and watches everyone else eat. Frosted Flakes and whole milk for Myrna. Raisin Bran and skim milk for Hugh. Cap'n Crunch, dry, for Jason. Shredded Wheat, left in brick form, with chocolate milk for Annabelle. Four boxes and three cartons.

"Tell me you like it," Mrs. Skelton says, as though she's made a standing rib roast. As though she wears a hairnet for General Mills or Kellogg's or Post. As though she knows the feel of a swollen udder in her manicured hands, a milking stool under her bony buttocks. *Tug, spray, tug, spray.* "Tell me I did good," she begs.

At department stores, Mrs. Skelton steals silk scarves because they're the easiest things to steal. They can slip into a tall boot, a gaping bra, a loose bun, a dieter's armpit. Mrs. Skelton justifies it by saying she'll someday use the scarves to perform a heroic deed. Like maybe lassoing a prizewinning pig from quicksand and giving up bacon. Mrs. Skelton goes to confessional booths and tapes tape recorders under the benches. Mrs. Skelton figures it's not a sin to listen to the sins of others if the sins of others are worse than hers.

The name of Mrs. Skelton's lipstick is Steamed Lobster. It's a wanton cerise that rings her saccharine soda cans, her mint-green toothbrush, the base of Mr. Skelton's penis. *Burning bush, burning bright. Tigress, tigress in the night.*

Mrs. Skelton never cooks. But still, a heat rises within her every night at dinner. While her silent family eats, she's pulling scarves out of thin air, one after another, like phrases of praise. *You did good. We like it. You did good. We like it.* The silks gather at her feet like colorful confessions. If she wanted, Mrs. Skelton could take the scarves and tie them all together and escape out a window, manicured and validated. She could make a fashionable noose and hang herself from a willow, a paper birch. Or she could take them, one by one, and poke them into her mouth, through her wanton, cerise lips like a reverse magic trick, and amaze everyone. Ta-da. Presto. Abracadabra.

Sara's sternum was a tuning fork, and the death had been a strike to her breastbone. Behind her flat face and ordinary dress was the eternal hum of terror. She hid it alongside a thin faith in a story-book God—animals two-by-two, a loaf made plural. Dinner parties only underscored these facts.

"What do I wear?" Sara asked Petra. What she meant was: *Press yourself against me until I fight for air.*

"Whatever you think," Petra said.

Petra was a lawyer for people who couldn't afford lawyers. Her work was kind, but she was less than. She possessed a commanding vacancy that filled Sara with despair and lust. The people at the party would be Petra's—people with meaningful jobs who remained unmoved by work or meaning. Sara had met them. They smelled of water, air—cold things no one could live without. Last time, they'd lounged about a solemn kitchen. On display were pomegranates split open like transplant organs, French pickles the size of babies' thumbs, sheets of transparent ham alongside the remains of a hand-fed sow. No one had eaten the pig. Before the party ended, it was tipped into a trash bag and curbed.

Sara saw doctors. They looked at her as if she spoke a lesser language. They pinched the bridges of their noses. They recommended Zoloft, vinegar tea, weightlifting. But mostly the pills. *There's a script for that,* they'd say. But Sara didn't want a script unless it told her the words her mouth should make.

Wallace Willis, the empath, came closest to curing Sara. His eyes were the color of blue ice—the pretend kind in the penguin part of zoos.

"Tell me your original fear," he said.

Sara remembered being an infant—her father shelving books from tallest to shortest, her mother sleeping, one arm dangling as if shot. "Baby powder," she said. It was a reminder everything was a cover-up.

"Well, now it's the death," Wallace Willis said. "The details, rather."

This was true. The death had settled in Sara like an anchor.

But the car, the limbs. People kept bringing up the details, stir-ring the sand. *I heard they found that over there. This over here.* People juggled their remarks like hot potatoes then tossed them at Sara. *Catch! Think fast!*

Sara wore a navy suit to the party. When she and Petra arrived, a woman named Jonas met them with two glasses of white liqueur. There were mint leaves floating on top. Jonas had on a gold camisole that clung to her nipples. Within each armpit glowed a suggestion of blonde hair. She showed her big teeth but didn't smile. "You made it," she observed.

In the kitchen, people stood with loose arms crossed. They said things like: *When did that become a thing?* At once, Sara knew only love would cure her—relentless, unbidden love that carried her until she could carry herself. It was a loan she could not qualify for. Ashamed, Sara swallowed her drink. The mint leaf stuck to the roof of her mouth. She could not remove it with her tongue.

"We were talking about the boy," a woman named Fels said.

"He climbs the Norway spruce," a woman named Regan said. "Out front."

Sara considered a row of tiny boiled eggs on the countertop.

"Pigeon," Fels said. "He was just adopted."

Regan yawned. "Is he white or Black or brown?"

"All three," Fels said.

That was the end of that. Regan asked about Fels's brass business. She sold antique candlesticks and the proceeds went to manatees. "They have no predators," said Fels. "The boats slice them because they aren't programmed for fear."

Sara went into the bathroom to remove the mint leaf. She

looked for pills as an explanation, but there were no pills. There wasn't even soap. Just a dish of oil that Sara rubbed between her palms but could not rinse off. When she came out, she heard one of the women say, *It is what it is.*

At camp, as a girl, Sara won a badge for asking the most questions about God. She kept it tucked in the bedsprings of the bunk above her. It was the first thing she saw when the bugle blew at dawn, the last thing she saw when the bugle blew at dusk. All summer long, her mother sent her clementines and crosswords. She rode a red horse named Jamcake. During canoeing, she let the life jacket bunch up under her chin so she could smell the mildew. The staff wore plastic gloves at suppertime. They reached into giant tins and brought out oily handfuls of potato chips. Sara's shins were spotted with green bruises. Her fingertips smelled forever of pine sap. At night, when the other girls slept, Sara placed her palm over the smooth mound between her legs until she saw the face of God. She had no need for love then.

At the dinner table sat ten white plates and ten short glasses filled with something the color of fog. Everyone stood behind their chairs and regarded the platter in the center. It held a gleaming pink slab that Sara thought might be tuna without skin or watermelon without rind. When she looked up, she saw him out the window. The boy, up the tree. On a limb, afraid.

"There he is," Sara gasped, pointing. "In the spruce."

The other nine stared at her blankly before they turned, slowly, to look.

"She says something," Fels shrugged. "The mother does."

At the base of the tree was a woman. Her arms went out

and up. Her mouth said words Sara needed to hear. Were they *I love you?* Were they *I'll leave you?* The other guests turned back to the table.

"People think they can't hear," Fels said. "But they can. They hear the boats perfectly fine, but they don't get out of the way."

Sara strained forward. The mother's mouth moved.

Jonas motioned to the reason they were all there. "Shall we?"

♡

The man was at the speed dating event dressed in pajama pants, gas station flip-flops, and a stretched-out Mount Rushmore T-shirt. Thomas Jefferson's face had been replaced with Lisa Simpson. The man's name tag said *HELIOTROPE*, but his real name was Travis.

"My friend Alicia dragged me here to get laid," Travis told the man across from him. His name tag said *BURT.* "No pressure, Burt."

Burt wore a three-piece suit, and he was sweating buckets. "I haven't sweat like this since the National Spelling Bee," Burt said, glancing at Lisa Simpson, then up at the ceiling. "Heliotrope. A hairy plant of the borage family known for aromatic flowers. A mirroring device used in surveying. Magenta, the color, also known as fuchsia. *F-U-C-H-S-I-A*, fuchsia. A bloodstone."

Heliotrope wasn't listening. He pulled a gray wad of gum from his mouth and stuck it to his index card of questions. "Chopsticks or fork? Window or aisle? Top or bottom?"

Burt patted a handkerchief over his forehead. "Cha-cha-cha," he stammered. "Chopsticks."

Heliotrope reached across the folding table and took Burt's hand. "Calm down," he said. "It's almost over."

"Okay," Burt said. "Okay."

Conveniently, the speed dating event was in the lobby of a hotel. When the timer dinged, Heliotrope and Burt went upstairs. They watched *The Simpsons* until Burt had had enough from the minibar to get an erection. Heliotrope took off his pajama pants but kept on his tee. Burt folded his suit and stalled for time until time ran out a second time. He looked at Heliotrope, he looked out the window. In his mind, someone played "Chopsticks." Heliotrope walked down an aisle. He carried heliotropes. Burt fed him groom's cake from a fork. They could drive off into the sunset, top down. They could honeymoon at the bottom of the Grand Canyon.

"Okay," Burt said. "*O-K*," Burt spelled.

Petal

Cynthia's heart trouble started in March, right after Todd and Thom came home for Easter. For seven days, she watched her grown sons slide around the house in suede shoes, drinking gimlets and observing their wives and children as if whale watching from a pier. Something collapsed in Cynthia after their visit: a valve, a vein, a dream. It was the first time she saw her offspring for what they were—indolent and indulged, careless with love—and the first time she saw herself for what she'd become: nothing more than a mother. Their mother.

There'd been a time in college when Cynthia thought she might make something of herself. Once, at a Sadie Hawkins dance, she abandoned her date for a full hour to kiss a female classmate in the broom closet, and afterward, a veil had lifted. What was stopping her from becoming a clarinetist, an equine vet, a wildlife photographer? She could learn to fly a plane. Across the Atlantic, alone! But then, summer came and with it, Ken. Ken had an attorney's temperament and plump wallet. His slim, clinical fingers felt like glass thermometers in and on Cynthia. He helped her to see that she was full of ridiculous, dangerous ideas, and by August, when Cynthia thought of herself learning to fly a plane, she cringed. So, she married Ken and had his children. Wore the diamonds, bobbed her hair.

In April, Cynthia's pulse went from fast to frenzied. She told her friend Patti about her heart problem, and Patti told her about Prima, the masseuse.

"She can fix anything. She cured Hat Fisher of the bad breast cancer."

"With massage?" Cynthia asked.

"She's magic," Patti said.

Cynthia decided to bring up Prima with Ken on their standing Thursday lunch date. Ken stared madly out at the Gulf. Cynthia forked through her crab salad as if looking for a solution. "There's this woman, a masseuse," she began, to which Ken stirred his chowder and replied, "Nelson caught a twenty-pound spadefish yesterday using a chicken tendon."

Prima had two buckets in her bathroom. One for bathing, one for waste. The landlord would send someone over to look at the clogs but not fix them. Prima was certain the people sent weren't plumbers but friends the landlord paid in painkillers to come and stand and shrug. "I'll send someone back about this," whoever was sent would say and then Prima and Mitch and Petal would wait and wait, and in the meantime they'd wash with a sponge from one bucket and piss and shit into another that they would empty, at night, into the storm drain of the complex's parking lot.

Still, Prima saw to it that their apartment was spotless. She spent money on three things only: Tang, canned pintos, and bleach. She bleached their buckets and hands and feet. She bleached their three towels and two sheets. They smelled like Olympic swimmers. "This is no way to live," Mitch would say. "It is this or death," Prima would answer, and then she would rub Mitch's shoulders until he saw butterflies and Petal, their beloved daughter, would squeal with glee, because she saw them too, and then they would sleep on the air mattress, together as one, a blessed trinity.

Mornings, Prima dressed in her mandarin shirt and apron. Her clients mistook her for Asian or Hispanic, but she was one-fourth Greek, one-fourth Romanian, one-fourth Icelandic, one-fourth Newarker. Mitch spent his days giving water to street dogs, letting them lick his eyes. It was all he could bring himself to do. As a child, his uncle had presented his penis to him in an open Bible. Mitch was spectacularly broken because of this and cried often. Prima loved him. Mitch loved Prima. They both loved Petal more than anything or anyone. To look at their daughter was to escape their reality. Her eyes were the color of acorns, her voice a June rain. She wore a red Goodwill dress and pink Goodwill shoes, and while Prima worked, Petal sat in an adjacent room stacking twelve plain wood building blocks.

At night, Mitch and Prima added to Petal's shrine using whatever items Prima had removed from her clients that day: delicate teacups painted with rosebuds, gold-plated platters intended for prime rib, turquoise belt buckles the size of telephone receivers, all matter of estate jewelry. These luxuries were grouped, piled really, on the chipped white tile of their apartment, alongside anything colorful or notable Mitch had found in the street. An orange plastic spoon, an empty rhinestone money clip, a dead green fly. Prayers were offered up to the gods of worth and worthlessness that Petal would never know fear or sadness, anger or regret, confusion or boredom, wealth or poverty. Her parents would see to that. This was present day, Texas. But it could have been past or future, Oregon or Saturn.

The unmarked clinic was at the far end of a strip mall, past a sub sandwich shop and a tattoo parlor. On the door, in small, gold, adhesive letters, was the word *PETAL*. Her friend Patti had told her: "All the door says is 'petal,'" and this scared Cynthia in a very primal way. She stood there in her Italian suit, staring at the letters, wondering if they had been applied by sight or by ruler. When Prima opened the door, Cynthia saw only Prima's deep, black eyes. In each iris floated a fleck of white that Cynthia knew was the reflection of her own timid face. Prima gave a firm bow and Cynthia entered. Inside the clinic, everything was slow and dim. It was like Cynthia was under gauze, in the shade. Like she was somewhere she didn't speak the language, a hammock in Vietnam, a boudoir in France.

"Here is a pen," Prima said. "Circle on the paper where you have the most pain."

Cynthia looked down at the paper. There was an outline of a sexless human body. She put an *X* over the left side of the empty chest where a heart could have been.

Prima took the paper and frowned. "So, do you want to love or be loved?"

Cynthia didn't know what to say. She was instantly aghast at herself. She should have marked the shoulders, a hamstring. She should have said her neck was stiff. Now she feared Prima would touch her breast, perform a spell.

"Is your heart dancing or limping?" Prima asked. "This will tell me what I need to know."

Cynthia shrugged like she didn't know, but she did. "I don't know," she said quietly. "Dancing, I guess."

Prima led her down a silent hallway and into a room where a radio played the sound of crickets and katydids. Prima pointed to a thick table wrapped in sheets. When Cynthia lay back on it, she was surprised to find it was heated. Prima blindfolded her and wrapped her feet in a hot, wet towel. For a while, Cynthia felt held hostage, by the linens, by her thoughts. Then her feet went from hot to warm and her breath went from quick to quiet. Her mind stilled to a glassy pool. Every nineteen seconds, she heard a single tree frog between the crickets and katydids. She pretended she was the frog. Prima brought her face down close to Cynthia's. She smelled mildly of cloves. "Do not answer, but ask yourself: Am I a rock in the river or a feather floating on top of it?"

Cynthia saw a cold rock at the bottom of her childhood lake. She and her cousin Bess were diving down to it, running their hands over its chartreuse moss, hair on a giant's skull. They dove down and came up, down and up in the cold lake until they crawled onto the wood dock and lay side by side in their bathing suits, holding hands in the sun. There was an electricity that ran down Bess's arm and up into Cynthia's, down Cynthia's throat and down between her legs until she shook madly and the electricity was sent back over to Bess who shook madly beside her. Cynthia could not remember if this had once happened or was happening now, on the table. Cynthia could not say if it was happening now, on the table, or only in her mind. The answers became unimportant next to the pleasure. Cynthia shook in the sun, listening for the frog, becoming who she should have been.

Prima could hardly keep pace. She pulled knotted strands of pearls from Cynthia's fingertips, silver saucers from her kneecaps. Her breasts were two velvet purses of coins, her flap of belly, a silk handbag. Turned over, Cynthia's spine became a row of pink bud vases, her shoulder blades two silver trays that slid out willingly and which Prima stacked quietly and carefully under the table with the rest of the trove. Turned back over, Cynthia had the same expression of someone who had died with her eyes open. Cynthia put her hand on her heart and paused. "It's fixed," she said, her eyes now darting left and right. "At least I think it is."

That night, Cynthia would go home to Ken and offer him love for the first time in a long time, and he would regard it like a meal he had not been served in years and was no longer able to eat. Prima would use the money Cynthia had paid her to buy Tang and canned pintos and bleach. She and Mitch and Petal would piss and shit into one bucket and bathe with bleach from another. They would eat their cold beans, drink their warm Tang. They would place Cynthia's treasures on Petal's altar and lay on the air mattress, together as one, their big eyes dotted with pearls and cups, knowing there were some things that could be fixed and some things that couldn't. And they were filled with joy because they knew the difference.

The Wind

For a short while, I lived in this city that was known for its wind. I know which city you're thinking of and it's not that one. Don't get hung up on which city it was—it's the wind that matters here more than the locale.

Anyway, for that short while, I had this apartment on the fourth floor of a newly renovated building, which sounds lovely, but really, it was just mediocre. The windows were old and drafty and made haunted house sounds when the wind kicked up, which was all the time. It was obvious that the renovations had been done on a budget. They were pinching pennies wherever and however they could. "They" meaning the owners, who I eventually ascertained were a group of wealthy fraternity guys just four years out of the fraternity. I ran into one of them once when I was sliding my little key into my mailbox in the lobby. The guy wore body cologne that conjured a rental car someone had recently been sick in. He had his Samsung on speaker and some girl on the other end was crying, yelling. *How could you? You're a real asshole, you know that?* The whole time he just stood there in the lobby, looking at me as if we knew each other, as if we both knew the girl and what she was capable of when unhinged. That was how it went for a few minutes: him smiling, him shaking his head, him pointing at his phone, him watching me open my mailbox like I was at a vending machine and he was next in line.

The only thing in my mailbox that day was a catalog for camping gear. I took a glance at its cover, then handed it to the guy with the blankest look I could muster. I knew he was the sort of person who would save a lot of money renovating an apartment building just so he, personally, could have extra spending money to buy things like high-end windbreakers that would go forever unused. As I walked away, the girl on the phone was still letting him have it, like she was making some headway, only she couldn't see the look on his face and I could.

But back to the penny-pinching. It was clear these owners were cheap. For example, they wallpapered the apartment building's hallways in a very loud, floral design to cover the imperfections in the drywall instead of just fixing the drywall. The wallpaper was outrageous. "Gaudy" would be the correct terminology. The whole corridor was plastered in poppies the size of pizzas. The poppies were in every imaginable color except for brown and gray and black and white and beige. In addition to being nauseating, bombastic even, the wallpaper was completely out of place geographically. This city was certainly no place for poppies, so if you are still stuck on which windy city I was in at the time, you can cross Miami off the list, though honestly, I don't even know how genuinely windy Miami is outside of hurricane season.

By the time the wallpaper went up, I had already signed a lease for a lonely one-bedroom in the building. Had I known that they, the fraternity guys, were going to mask things, I would have shopped around, but by the time the poppies bloomed over the shoddy drywall, they already had a deposit out of me, as well as my signature. The next quick fix I encountered was indoor-outdoor carpeting over decrepit tile in the rear entrance, then silver spray paint over some stainless steel snafu in the elevator. On the day I moved in, I noticed my refrigerator door handle had been glued on. The glue had oozed out and dried around the handle like hardened peanut butter. However, I was in this windy city to go to art school, to study ceramics. Would a real artist complain about a glued-on refrigerator handle? Probably not. I wanted to be a real artist very badly, so I kept my mouth shut about the handle. I tried to love the handle and the way it was attached in the hopes it would hurry up and make me into the person I wanted to be.

Art school did not go well. Things started off hopeful, idealistic. Or at least I did. I had grand plans for my first ceramic series. I wanted to make eight to ten glazed pipes (smoking pipes, not plumbing pipes), with a different glazed animal coming out of each one. The pipes were going to be quite large, because the animals were going to be life-sized woodland creatures. Squirrels, rabbits, opossums, etc. The title of the series was going to be *Put That in Your Pipe and Smoke It.* The whole project was meant to be a metaphor about parents and how they always wanted their children to accept whatever cards they'd been dealt. It was about how parents never wanted to empathize or sympathize with their children. About how they just wanted their children to smile, shake it off. *Persevere.* The woodland animals were inserted into the whole thing as innocent sacrifices.

When I presented the proposal to my class in the form of large pencil sketches, everyone sat for a few minutes in excruciating silence. Finally, one guy weighed in. He thought my pipes looked like musical instruments. "Are they saxophones?" he asked. The guy had a piercing that went straight through the center of his nose, the bone I think, and could have easily been mistaken for a roofing nail. I had secretly found him attractive during orientation and ever since had been having a recurring erotic dream about him, with one of the recurrences occurring the night before my proposal.

In the dream, the guy and I walked along the lake—again, not the city you're thinking of—and I was wearing nothing more than a thong and a Gap sweatshirt. You know how some couples walk along with their hands in one another's back pockets? Well, that's what we were doing, so you can guess where his hand was given what I had on. It was a very sexy dream—not at all self-conscious—but, when the guy started in on the saxophone thing, and then someone else said *Clarinets!* and someone else said, *Raccoon!* And then someone shouted, *Juvenile!* and then the guy who started it all yelled, *Cartoony!* I might as well have been standing there in my underwear. I just fell completely apart. I didn't fall apart on the outside, just the inside. Ultimately, it wasn't about my art. It's never the thing that precedes the crash. For me, the falling apart was about my parents. Not so much how they treated me, but how they treated each other. That was what came up when my parent-related project got laughed at: Francesca and Jack Blanchard.

*

There was a lone, exhausted therapist at the art school. His name was Edmund, and he had an office that had once been a coat closet. Technically it was still a coat closet. There was a metal rod for clothing that ran above his tiny metal desk. He sat on the metal desk while I sat on a metal chair. The only other thing on Edmund's desk, besides Edmund, was a red plastic basket. The woven sort that a hamburger and fries might be served in. Or maybe fish and chips. Except this basket was filled with complimentary condoms. Off-brand ones, to make matters worse, and the whole time I talked to Edmund, I just stared at the lousy, unreliable condoms and imagined how many people were getting pregnant at art school.

"My mother told me this thing once that I can't forget," I told Edmund. "She said: 'If I don't need enough from him, your father threatens to kill me. But if I need too much from him, your father threatens to kill himself.'"

"Shit," Edmund said. "That is some heavy shit, Claudette." My name is Claudette, which no one ever expects. Is 'Claudette' hot and French? Or is 'Claudette' your waitress at the Waffle House? This is the million-dollar question and always will be. "That's a pretty crazy thing for a mother to tell her kid, right?"

I shrugged. I shrugged at every session. This was the only thing Edmund and I talked about. Literally just this statement of my mother's. I'd come in, sit down on my metal surface, he would sit down on his metal surface. He'd reach up behind himself and toy with the metal closet rod. I'd stare at the fried-clam basket of budget condoms, and we'd pick up where we left off: still discussing those two sentences of my mother's.

"I don't know," I'd say. "I don't think it's heavy shit, really, though it *has* stuck with me. I think it's just the truth. My parents were textbook codependents. Their emotional states were completely dependent on each other. So, what my mother said was utterly true. And I always find it insane that people panic at the truth. People have always been, like 'Your mother shouldn't have said something like that to her kid,' and I've always been, like 'What? The truth?'"

Edmund considered this for a long time. I got the feeling most students he saw at art school came to him to talk about depression and desperation. You can only make so many pipes filled with animals before you start questioning the meaning of life. I was only a few weeks into my first semester, and I'd ditched the pipe project to make nine asymmetrical salad bowls. I think I was a relief for Edmund in many ways. Every week when I came in, I could tell that he was really trying to unpack what my mother had said and what sort of effect it had had, and it made me think that Edmund had something similar going on in his background. He was professional enough not to bring up his own life, but he was always dressed in a neat corduroy button-down. He had thinning hair and a discernible part. He always stopped three or four times during our session to clean his glasses with his shirttail. I wore khaki cargo pants and pearl earrings. I did not have a roofing nail through my nose. I think we were similar. Artistic but not *artistic*. Normal but not *normal*. I think I was a soft place for Edmund to land once a week. That said, eventually I quit seeing Edmund because I felt like my session became more about him than me, and I eventually quit art school because I was so sad. By November, I was broken and hollow and in need of good therapy, and Edmund was just a regular, bewildered guy in a closet, unknowingly getting people pregnant.

My parents came up to the city that was windy to bring me

home. I was too old for them to do that sort of thing: pack me up and chauffeur me around—I was graduate student, for Pete's sake—but the city had a Ritz and, ever since the scratch-off, my parents were suckers for a Ritz. When my father had won fifty grand a few years back, the one thing he and my mother had agreed on was to spend all of it on Ritzes. So, when I announced I was dropping out, they came to my apartment with a Ritz reservation and a small U-Haul with a couple of movers they had paid.

"Jesus," my dad said. "This wallpaper. No wonder you have to get the hell out of here."

My mother just stared out my one apartment window, while the movers and I wrapped my clay bowls in bubble wrap. "Jack!" she gasped. "I see a rat! In the middle of the day!"

That night, the U-Haul went back south, through the cornfields, and my parents got two king rooms on the highest floor of the hotel. The wind was really howling that night. On our way to and from dinner outside of the Ritz, we saw a revolving door that had shattered at an ATM. We also saw a man trying to walk a terrier on a leash and the terrier was airborne, a kite. My mother had had three glasses of wine at dinner, and she wanted to laugh about that with the man—his airborne dog—but the man did not think it was funny at all. And to be honest, the wind was so intense that talking was pointless. My father was holding onto a streetlamp and my mother was holding onto him. I had to pick my way from newspaper box to newspaper box. All I could hear was the wind and the lake, which sounded the same.

I went up to my hotel room alone and filled the bathtub. It was only filled halfway when I saw: the water was sloshing back and forth like I was on a cruise ship and not in a skyscraper. That's how windy it was. The skyscraper was rocking back and forth, so my bathwater was rocking back and forth. It was so unnerving, I could not bring myself to get in the tub. Instead, I got into bed and turned out all the lights and put on a movie with a lot of special effects to distract me from the fact that I was in a building that was bending, swaying.

The next day, I moved back to my hometown. Within a year, I had met and married a normal man who was not artistic at all. We lived a very uneventful life until I decided to get back into ceramics after our only son turned three. "Ceramics?" my husband said. "What's the point of ceramics?"

It was a terrible question that raised the very real possibility that he was a terrible person, but it was also a question that couldn't be satisfactorily answered, which made him think he had a point. I liked the feel of wet clay, the satisfying sheen of glaze. I liked producing an ambiguous, flirtatious shape that made people mildly uncomfortable. But these were things, reasons, that didn't pay bills or feed mouths or end wars.

Still, I went on and got back into ceramics. For my first project, I made over one hundred little pipes with tiny insects popping out of them. I entered them into a local art competition under the title *Pipe Down* and won a thousand dollars. Our son, nearing four by then, was so proud of me. I gave him the best pipe in the whole series, a shiny lavender one with a tomato-red cicada emerging from it. On the night of the show, he put it under his pillow at bedtime, and later, after my son had fallen asleep, my husband pulled me into our bedroom and tried to strangle me.

"A thousand dollars," he seethed, shaking me by the neck. His hands went from tight to loose, tight to loose, like he couldn't decide if I was worth the trouble, the consequences. "I bet you think you're something else now." He sounded like he

was going to cry. "A thousand dollars for clay. A real somebody."
Eventually he went limp and stopped and ended up sleeping in
the basement, on a camping cot. To be safe, I went and slept in
my son's bed, beside my son.

The next morning at breakfast, my husband walked through
the kitchen without making eye contact. "We got wild, huh?"
he said.

I didn't say anything back. I was unable to form words in my
head or with my mouth. In that moment, I had never before felt
the way I felt. I was outside of myself, spooning eggs onto my
son's plate, trying to figure out if I had died or not. Was I a ghost?
I was somewhere between my body and the ceiling. I couldn't
imagine how to get my feet back into my feet.

After my husband went to work, I called a sitter. I didn't
know what I was doing or why, but when she arrived, I got into
my car and started driving. The ceramics from the night before
were still in the backseat, and I could hear them sliding around in
a cardboard box. As I drove, all I could think of was that everything was the opposite of what it seemed to be. I'd thought a
renovated apartment would be nice. I'd thought art school would
be friendly. I'd thought a normal man would be safe. Behind the
poppies, it was all pockmarks.

I drove all the way to that city. The windy one. I spent my
thousand dollars of prize money on a room at the Ritz, and I
requested it be on the highest floor possible. When I got upstairs,
I stripped down and put on the complimentary robe and filled up
the bathtub. I sat on the side of the tub for a long time and waited.
I was about to give up, but around midnight, it happened. The
water started sloshing. To the back of the tub and then toward
the drain. To the back and the drain, to the back and the drain.

That was when I got my room key and went out to the elevator. I rode all the way downstairs in my robe and I went into the hotel bar. It is surprisingly easy to convince a man to come back to your hotel room when you're wearing a robe in a public place at midnight. It was obvious that I could have had any of them sitting there, but I chose the one who was alone at a table with his laptop. He looked something like Edmund. Normal but not *normal*. I sat down across from him and leaned over the small cocktail table. "I have something I need someone to see," I said to him. "In my room." The man looked around at all the men looking at him, then he looked at me. After a pause, he closed his laptop. "Please," I said. The man blinked and swallowed. "Okay," he said.

Back in my room, in my bathroom, we both just stood there staring at the tub. We watched the water go left and right, left and right. The man was quiet. I don't think it was because he was as amazed as I was. I think it was because he was a decent person trying to be polite. He probably thought I had snapped, but I turned to face him anyway. How could I make him understand that everything was the opposite of what it pretended to be? I needed one person to see behind the flowers.

"So, this is what you brought me up here to see?" the man asked. "The water?"

"Yes," I said. I reached for both of his hands and took them in mine. "But it's not the water you're looking at. It's the wind."

Brain, Brian

Marvin's brain tumor is the size of an unshelled walnut. His doctor, who wears Crocs the color of bile, has told Marvin and Marvin's wife, Cathy, that he plans on removing the tumor with a knife that's not really a knife but a beam of light. When the surgery was first explained, Marvin saw a hot spatula cutting cold cheesecake, but now that the operation is tomorrow, he keeps seeing a red, plastic flashlight pointed at a dense, winter wood. *Who goes there?* he hears the surgeon call out, gleefully. *Make yourself known!*

The neurosurgeon is as young as Marvin's son, Brian. Brian no longer speaks to Marvin. Brian lives in Arizona with a girl Marvin and Cathy have never met but whose name is Begonia. They've seen a picture of their son and this girl. A dog that looked like a coyote was also in the picture. "Who wants a cartoon for a dog?" Marvin asked Cathy. "Who wants a houseplant for a girlfriend?"

Marvin was a terrible father, but the tumor has lessened the reality of this. The larger the tumor grows, the better father Marvin was. And the faster Marvin walks, the faster the tumor grows. Which is why, every morning, he goes to the mall in his big white shoes, the ones that look like loaves of junk bread, and walks eight thousand steps. He walks from one anchor store to the other—fourteen times, back and forth—and as he does, he recalls things he thought about doing with Brian as things he actually did. Camping under a swirl of stars. Shooting clay pigeons. Making cowboy beans in a cast-iron frying pan. "There's Orion," he hears himself say. "More pintos?"

In the early morning mall, the managers raise the gated storefronts with much audible ado. The mall fountains sputter to life. Together, the fountains and the gates sound like static, and Marvin's mind becomes the roaring space between canyon walls. He passes stores. There's Queen B., Banana Pants, Mr. Stupid. There's bright and beautiful SprayBaby. He stares at the things for sale and cannot remember what they are for. He imagines a pair of underwear on a potted begonia. Women's yellow overalls on a coyote. A whoopee cushion as a map of Arizona. Marvin moves his big white shoes faster. He forgets Brian's thin shoulders and crystalline singing voice. He forgets Brian's pitiful deer eyes, his milkweed hair. Instead, Marvin remembers throwing a football that was never thrown, laughing at a joke that was never cracked.

At the end of Marvin's morning walk is Sprinkles, the ice cream kiosk. If Marvin times it right, he takes his last step when Dashel, the ice cream boy, flips over the *OPEN* sign. "Good morning, Marvin," Dashel says. "The usual?" Marvin's excitement is such that he can only nod. His head nods and the tumor nods, and fireworks go off in Marvin's mind—red and green and violet.

Dashel scoops the vanilla while Marvin watches. It's a sphere of snow rolled through a pristine field, the belly of a snowman that Marvin and Brian did and didn't build. Dashel rolls the vanilla through rainbow sprinkles, a brain dragged through artificial memories. *I helped Brian make a papier-mâché sarcophagus for Ancient History class. I built Brian a tree house with a trapdoor and pulley system. I told Brian I loved him. I told Brian I was proud of him.*

Dashel puts the ice cream into a paper bowl and places a shelled walnut on top. He hands the ice cream to Marvin, and Marvin goes and sits on a bench by the fountains. Every morning, he sits there until the ice cream has melted and the sprinkles have bled and all that remains is the walnut—floating in gray matter—and Marvin, quite pleased with himself. Tomorrow is another story. Tomorrow the doctor will remove the walnut with a knife made of light. Tomorrow he will have his brain back. Today he has Brian.

The Owner

Nina and her husband, Harry, got a good deal on the house. It was a charming bone-colored Cape Cod that seemed to have an agreement with the elements. All over, it was tilted and weathered but also sturdy—petrified, almost. They never met the owner. "He's in a retirement situation now," the realtor said, unprompted, twice during the closing. She said it in a plain, firm way that Nina and her husband did not question. Perhaps he was playing golf. Perhaps he was in hell.

On the first night in the house, Nina dreamed of the owner. He sat in a canvas chair in the desert. To his left was a stunted palm tree. To his right, a beach ball that didn't roll away. He gazed out over an expanse of red sand. He wore a gas mask, but Nina could still hear what he said. "I left you something. Did you find it?"

Nina woke with a jolt. Beside her, Harry breathed serenely.

She rose and went into the bathroom and opened the medicine cabinet. She wanted an aspirin, but all she found was a Band-Aid tin—the vintage, metal kind—and inside of that a single white bead. Nina inspected the bead. It was the size of a large pea with a tidy, drilled hole. She put the bead back into the tin and the tin back into the cabinet. She drank from the faucet. When she returned to bed, she could not sleep. She kept seeing the gas mask, the stunted palm. She kept trying to move the beach ball with her thoughts.

In the morning, while Nina stood in front of the toaster, Harry came up behind her and kissed the nape of her neck. When she turned around, he wasn't there. "Harry?" she called. "Was that you?" Harry didn't answer, even when she called out again. Nina stood, frowning, until her toast popped up. In that short time, to her surprise, she was able to recall every argument she and Harry had ever had. There had been problems with money and romance, fertility and drinking. Right after they'd first married, there'd also been a woman. A neighbor named Pearl who visited three or four times a week with something from her garden: profane-looking cucumbers, swollen purple tomatoes, fistfuls of fragrant basil. She was good-natured about everything and everyone. There was always a ladybug in her hair. Nina had never seen Harry so happy. He accepted everything Pearl brought without once looking down at what Pearl brought. "You look at her too much," Nina had said. "Maybe you could learn a thing or two," Harry had said back.

Nina hadn't thought about Pearl in a long time. She was filled with a sudden sadness. She left the toast in the toaster to grow stale. She went back to the bedroom and curled on the bed. This time, when she dreamed of the owner, he had two gas masks—one on his face and one that he held out for Nina. The beach ball was still in the same place. The palm tree was nearly dead. When Nina woke up, she discovered two more white beads on the floor, side by side.

Every day, in an unexpected place, Nina found another bead. She found one in the lint screen of the dryer. One in the soil of a cactus she repotted. One at the bottom of a bowl of tomato soup. One day, she coughed a single cough and a bead appeared on her tongue. Nina kept all the beads. She stored them in the Band-Aid tin. Sometimes she shook the tin to hear the noise it made. *Gotcha, gotcha, gotcha*, it said.

Nina and Harry weren't happy in the new house; they bickered all the time. The only thing that brought Nina hope were the beads and the dreams, though neither of those made any real sense to her. She slept excessively. Harry came home later and later in the evenings smelling of beer, cigars, perfume. When he slept, he no longer breathed serenely. Instead, he snored, causing Nina's dreams to take an urgent turn. There was a loud, new factory in the desert, churning out clouds of navy smoke, and she and the owner would sit in the canvas chairs wearing gas masks looking at it.

"What are they making?" she'd ask him.

"It's not what you think," he'd say.

Then Nina would wake up and drink from the faucet and discover another bead. Maybe pressed into the soft, pink meat of her heel. Maybe near the sink drain, in the tiny groove that kept it from drowning.

*

When Nina had forty beads, she spread them on the kitchen table after Harry had gone to work. She put twenty in one row, then twenty in a row below it. She pretended they were teeth. While she arranged the beads, someone came and kissed her on the nape of her neck, but this time she did not turn to see who it was. That night, Harry was the latest he had ever been.

"Where have you been?" Nina asked.

"It's not what you think," he said.

Harry swayed at the foot of the bed. Nina felt her hands begin to shake. "I don't like this house," she said. "I wish we'd never bought it."

Harry shook his head. "I knew this would happen."

Nina's eyes filled with tears. She lay back in bed. She heard Harry leave the room and then the house. Then she let herself cry until she was there, in the desert with the owner, reaching out for the gas mask and putting it on.

"What happened to the palm tree?" Nina asked.

"It died," said the owner.

"And the beach ball?"

"It rolled away."

Nina didn't want to sit in the canvas chair. "Let's walk to the factory," she said. "Let's see what they make."

The owner said nothing, but he got up and off they went, across the red sand together. The factory was larger and louder than life and made of black glass. When they got up to it, Nina pressed her face against it but couldn't see inside. All she could see was her own reflection, her face in its gas mask, and the owner standing behind her, his face in his.

"Look what I have," he said. He held up something small and square and gave it a shake. *Gotcha, gotcha, gotcha.* Nina froze, petrified. She watched as the owner opened the tin and brought out the beads. All forty were now on a string, and he placed them around her neck, stopping to stroke her nape, before he fastened them. Nina placed one palm on the factory's black glass, the other at the hollow of her throat. As the necklace grew tighter, the factory grew louder. She thought to call for Harry, but she could not speak, could not breathe. She could only see the image of her masked face and that of the owner's looking back at her. Her vision began to dim but not before she saw: a final bead—a red one—on the lens of the owner's mask. Moving, gently. A ladybug.

North Colorado

Linda couldn't eat shellfish. Well, she wouldn't die if she did (it wasn't an allergy per se), it's just that if and when she did eat it, she had these vivid, lucid dreams that fell somewhere between bizarre and terrifying, not to mention: sleep paralysis. The last time Linda went out with Rick and the kids to the Tugboat, she thought, *Oh, what the heck, I'm gonna get the scampi!* only that night to dream her hands had turned into cats.

Having cats for hands may not sound like a nightmare, but wait until you're leaning over the most true-to-life clawfoot tub ever, and the sun is filtering through the eyelet curtains in a hyperrealistic way, and you're bathing your infant son who looks more like your infant son than your real infant son ever did, and the only way to keep him from slipping under the bubbles and turning blue is to grab him with two hissing calicos.

Those cats had torn up Bradley terribly, nearly shredding his precious newborn skin. As an added bonus, Linda had lain in bed petrified after waking, eyes open, her mouth opening and closing like a grounded koi, her body pinned and frozen as though a steel safe had been set on her sternum. After that nocturnal misadventure, Linda swiftly retaliated: *Scampi? Off the list.* Followed by clams casino and oysters Rockefeller and bacon-wrapped scallops and squid. What a shame; Linda just adored squid, but not if it meant dreaming she'd been hired to drive the Wienermobile cross-country to elementary schools only to discover the Wienermobile was made of actual pork. In that one, Linda only got fifteen minutes outside of Columbus before vultures swarmed the vehicle like horror movie cockroaches and ate the entire thing out from under her, leaving her to hitchhike on the side of I-70 in a lace slip until a pumpkin farmer from Zanesville rescued her. For that doozy, just two bites of fried calamari had been to blame.

For nine months now, Linda had been shellfish-free. But then, just last night, all the gals got together for bunko over at Roberta's and Linda fell off the wagon. It wasn't her fault; everyone brought something to snack on and something to sip on (which usually meant a dozen ladies with a dozen bottles of drugstore chardonnay and a dozen cheap foil pans of artichoke dip), but DeeDee Sykes had tried her hand at some newfangled buffalo bites and everyone'd gone mad. Especially Linda. After she devoured about eight of them and asked for the recipe, DeeDee informed her they were made with mayonnaise and Tabasco and puff pastry and—*if you're lucky enough to find it fresh, girls!*— Dungeness.

"Crab?" Linda stammered, turning white and holding her heart.

"Oh, Jesus, Linda," DeeDee grabbed her by the shoulders.

"I thought you heard me tell everyone they were crab. Were you in the bathroom or something? Jesus, Linda. Don't die on me." DeeDee nearly dropped to the floor in repentance. "Who has an Epi?" she shouted. "We need an Epi!"

"I'm not allergic," Linda managed, but the look on her face was so pale and panicked that no one believed her. They thought the toxins had already taken hold and were causing her to lie. They dug through their purses like the good mothers they were and produced various antidotes: liquid Benadryl, chewable Benadryl, Visine, Pepto-Bismol, a rectal thermometer, six crayons, a fistful of tampons, and some Mad Libs. "Stop," Linda insisted. "Please."

DeeDee didn't let up. "What's first? Hives? Heartburn? Anaphylactic? Dr. Flynn is down the street on Maple. Someone call Kent. Roberta, do you have the Flynns' number?"

"Oh, stop it," Linda said. "He's an ophthalmologist, for God's sake. I'm not allergic. It's just . . ." She hesitated, afraid of sounding foolish. "It's just. Shellfish gives me weird dreams."

The bunko gals breathed a collective sigh. "Oh, thank goodness," DeeDee collapsed from the waist up on the granite kitchen island.

"Honey," Brenda Brock said, an unlit Marlboro Light bouncing between her lips (she'd quit smoking lit ones six years ago). "It's not the shellfish. It's perimenopause. That's where the dreams come from." She offered Linda another buffalo bite with a raised eyebrow. "Hate to break it to you."

Linda gave everyone a round of nods and smiles to reassure them it wasn't curtains. But she couldn't focus on the bunko game. She made very little in the way of conversation and could scarcely crack a smile, not even when Brenda Brock had everyone in hysterics, once again, with her "giant clam theory." "That's all we are ladies. A giant clam the kids crawl out of and the men crawl into." *Ha ha ha! Clink, clink! Ha ha ha ha HA!*

In the end, Linda only put back about a glass of wine, which was very unlike her when the gals got together. Rick usually could expect to get lucky on bunko nights, and he was waiting for just this when she came home at ten. "You're early," he smiled from his side of the bed, patting her pillow.

Linda dropped her purse and put the barely touched bottle of chardonnay on the nightstand and flopped on top of the bedspread, still clothed, to confess to her husband. "I ate shellfish," she almost sobbed. "DeeDee made these crab things that tasted like chicken things."

"Oh," Rick said, removing his hand from her pillow and picking up his library book. "Well, look on the sunny side. Maybe you'll have a dream that you're the Statue of Liberty. Or that the dog shits Häagen-Dazs."

"Don't be crude, Rick." Linda raised up her hips to remove her belt, then she kicked her shoes to the floor and rolled over, still wearing her spangled jeans and floral V-neck, already defeated. It'd be just like her to go out of this world in an impulse outfit. To die or go mad before she'd seen the Eiffel Tower or gotten her thighs the way she wanted them or convinced Rick to ballroom dance or explained the ins and outs of credit cards and venereal disease to the kids. "Who knows what I'm in for." She put a pillow on her head, on the off chance the dreams came from without and not within. She had no idea how she'd ever fall asleep.

But Linda does fall asleep and Linda does dream.

She dreams about two girls she admired in childhood—

Amy Weingartner, a leggy drum majorette who dazzled the entire junior high before moving midyear to the desert, and Dana Hoop, the broad-shouldered lesbian counselor at Camp Cherrywood who could hit bullseye after bullseye blindfolded.

Amy and Dana and Linda stand on top of a mountain range—it could be the Rockies or the Himalayas or the Alps, but it's not: it's someplace much more impressive, empyrean. Linda thinks it might be called North Colorado, but she's not sure how she knows this. The sky's a shocking azure. Violet patches of asters interrupt the snowfields. Here and there, apparitions appear and disappear—a unicorn, James Gandolfini, Linda's dead aunt Joan? (Linda's dead aunt Joan!), Charlotte Brontë, a harp seal.

"Should we let the babies in?" Amy asks Dana.

Dana adjusts the giant golden quiver on her back; it must be the size of Maine. "Hell yeah," she says.

Linda doesn't know yet if she's visible or invisible to them, so gives a meek *ahem*. Dana gives her the side-eye. "You comin' with, cupcake?" Dana asks Linda.

"She's coming with," Amy answers for her.

They march like Amazonians out over the snowfields—Amy in her gold majorette getup and Dana in her fringed leather jumper. Their massive legs are a display of carved brawn—Amy's alabaster, Dana's mahogany. Linda can suddenly recall the scientific names for all the thigh muscles: *Sartorius, rectus femoris, vastus medialis, gracilis, semitendinosus.* She memorized them in her first year of med school when she'd wanted to become an obstetrician. Then she'd gotten pregnant with Hope and settled for nursing school. Then she'd gotten pregnant with Bradley and settled for working the front desk at a pediatrician's. Then she'd gotten pregnant with Molly and settled for making hair accessories at the kitchen table with a glue gun.

God, she thinks. *I'm such a failure. How did I end up crafting ribbon barrettes? Loser,* she thinks again. *Loser, loser, loser.*

"Oh, get over it!" Dana turns and shouts at Linda, reading her mind. "You're not a goddamn loser. You're here, aren't you? Do you know how hard it is to get HERE?" Dana draws an arrow the size of the Seattle Space Needle from her quiver and waves it around at all there is to see. Linda cowers. "You've got a big job coming up, Linz. Amy and I can't do it without you. Lives depend on it."

Suddenly, there's the sound of a whale breaching. Amy stops and points with her baton. Dana gets down on her knees, the earth trembling in response, and reaches out over a cliff and into a green ocean that Linda's just now noticing to pull up a humpback. Dana moves the top of her jumper to one side and begins to breastfeed it. "You're a god now, Linda. I'm a god, Amy's a god. We're all three gods. You better get used to it." The whale writhes like a brook trout in Dana's arms. She consoles it, makes sure it's latched on, stares out at the ocean while she gives of herself.

Dana's breasts are equally manlike and womanlike. From one angle they look pectoral, from another buxom. The same holds true for her shoulders and hips and for Amy's breasts and shoulders and hips. Linda is afraid to look down at her own body. She has the instant awareness that she might have giant testicles AND lady parts. She focuses on the whale instead, how it's molded itself against Dana's body the same way Hope and Bradley and Molly did hers, convincing her to give up her dreams for decades of wiping them.

"You're both," Dana says, breaking the suspense. "Male and female." Linda doesn't know what to say. She moves her feet

194

further apart to allow for airflow and denial. *How is that possible?* "Anything's possible here," Dana responds. "Anyone, everything." At this, the humpback has finished. She pulls it from her chest and tosses it back into the sea. "Onward!" she shouts.

"Onward!" Amy concurs.

The women go forth. Linda jogs to keep up. She starts feeling better about herself and her lot, in the sunlight, in the snow, with her coexisting balls and breasts. She starts to uncower, to look around, to take in the magnificence. North Colorado is where it's at! Look at that firmament, those asters, that blue-green valley below. It's realer than real. When she sees a rainbow arching over a distant snowfield, it occurs to her that she's been trying to get back to this place her whole life. "I'm back!" she hears herself shout. "I'm finally back!"

Amy and Dana exchange a knowing look and snicker. Then Amy, as if to further stun Linda, raises her gold baton and twirls it. Birds and insects and small woodland creatures shoot from its tips and run scurrying to populate the mountainsides.

"Your baton," Linda stammers. "Does it, like . . ."

"Make shit?" Amy finishes for her again. "You bet."

Linda smiles broadly. "So where are we going?"

Amy spins a marmot from her baton and then points with it. "To the portal," she says. "To deliver the babies. And then, if there's time, maybe the big-hearts."

When Linda wakes up she's more paralyzed than ever. For a good twenty minutes she lays there koi-gaping, considering her options if DeeDee's buffalo bites have rendered her permanently immobile. Rick is decent with housework but terrible with caregiving. They'll have to hire someone to change her diapers, to feed her soup, to sponge her armpits. Rick will have an affair. Her children will stop bringing friends over; they'll become distant, dysfunctional. All because of Dungeness.

But soon enough, Linda's limbs lighten and the shame falls away and she is back to herself. Except, not really. As she goes about her morning routine of make the lunches, wake the kids, make the breakfast, wake the kids again, find the shoes, tear off the bedsheets and yell, her mind plays the dream on repeat. It refuses to fade like a normal one, but instead grows more vivid, more real than the world around her. By late morning, in the supermarket's dog food aisle, Linda can recall with unsettling clarity the rainbow over the snowfield. *That's where I belong. That's where I'm from*, she thinks. *I must get back.* In a surge of panic and passion, Linda abandons her half-full shopping cart by the kitty litter and runs to the seafood counter, where she selects a briny container of sad-looking scallops as if her life depends on it.

At home, she broils them without butter or salt and swallows six in succession. She knows she should be at the pharmacy and the bank and at the uniform store buying the kids new cardigans for the semester, checking to see when her mammogram's due, brushing the dog's teeth, balancing her checkbook, watering the philodendron, braiding those barrettes the junior cheerleaders go gaga for, but instead she climbs into bed and sets the alarm for afternoon carpool and tries to fall asleep. After twenty minutes of staring at the ceiling, Linda drinks from the chardonnay still on the nightstand. Just a glass. Then two. Then almost three, until she is out. And dreaming.

At 2:45 the alarm goes off and Linda wakes, paralyzed. She koi-gapes for a while, terrified. Not because she can't move her arms or legs or reach the alarm or utter a word, but because her dream has had nothing to do with Amy or Dana or North Colorado. There were no soaring peaks and patches of frosted fuchsia and nursing whales. There was no imperative mission to deliver babies and big-hearts. The dream had been little more than a brisk tour of Beverly Hills, on camels with Patti LaBelle. Linda and Patti had gone through the drive-thru at In-N-Out Burger and ordered two Double-Doubles but hadn't been able to reach them from atop the animals. That was when Patti's "On My Own" had overlapped with the scheduled Marimba on Linda's phone.

After a few minutes, Linda regains her movement. She sits up and holds her head. She is tipsy and devastated and needs to cram her mouth with Altoids and Advil before picking up the kids, but before she does, she calls DeeDee Sykes. "DeeDee? It's Linda," she says. "Can you send me a link to those buffalo crab bites? Yes, the recipe. Yes, I know it has crab in it. Yes, now. I need to make them tonight."

Between two mountain peaks, Amy and Dana wait for Linda on a blue-shadowed snowfield. Amy spins her baton in greeting and snowshoe hares and peppered-fur pikas and one cumbersome alpine ibex explode forth before scurrying to distant expanses of bluegrass. Dana waves one hand hello as her other cradles a nursing beluga. This time around, Linda starts off swaggering. North Colorado is so the bee's knees, she can't stop singing—*This land was made for me and me.* She takes in deep breaths of pristine air, her lungs billowing like clipper sails within her. She can feel the swing of her scrotum, the shapeshifting nature of her breasts. Linda looks down and notes that she's wearing minty green doctor's scrubs. She touches her forehead and discovers a headlamp. As she approaches the snowfield, she sees that between Amy and

Dana there's something of a small cave. She stops and cocks her head. Where the two mountains meet, the landscape resembles a woman reclining, her legs bent. The cave is no cave after all, but an entrance. A portal. A birth canal. Is this what's at the end of the rainbow? A vagina?

"You're just in time," Amy says, pointing at the tiny grotto with her baton. "Do you see?"

Dana throws the beluga over a cliff, puts a giant, warm hand on Linda's back. "Take a look, cupcake. This is why we need you."

The opening is much smaller than Linda, but still the size of a redwood hewn in half. She presses an eye to the cave, a leviathan peering into a keyhole. Inside? The entire universe. Galaxies and nebulae and shooting stars and planets. There's Mars, a maraschino cherry. And Jupiter, a scoop of raspberry swirl. And also Earth. It's as small as a party favor, a swirly, rubber bouncy ball that Linda momentarily imagines plucking from the sky and tossing.

"Bad idea, Linz," Dana says, poking her in the back with an arrow's dull end. "But tempting, I know."

Linda turns around, now unnerved. "Is that the real Earth?"

Amy and Dana laugh long and loud. Their mirthful roaring sends birds flying in from all directions, a sudden Technicolor migration. Clouds of macaws and flamingos, cardinals and parakeets fly in patterns about the sky, bright paper cards flipped by invisible stadium crowds. Linda asks again. "No, seriously. Where am I?"

"Why, Linda," Dana points at the scrubs and headlamp. "Can't you see? You're at work."

Linda looks at Amy then Dana then Amy. "That's all?"

"Yes, damn it, that's all," Dana says. "And you better get to it."

Linda peers again into the portal. A line of celestial figures expands out into the distant stars. "I see them!" she exclaims.

"Are they babies?" Amy asks. "The first ones should be babies."

Linda confirms. The first thousand or so are indeed babies. They are plump and smiling, naked and flawless with both male and female parts, cooing at stars, grasping at passing asteroids. Some appear as young as newborns, others as old as five. But their most remarkable features are their hearts—bright pink auras that pulse to a synchronized heartbeat, propelling them forward like sea creatures in the dark deep. Before Linda knows it, there's one pulsing at the mouth of the cave.

"It's delivery time," Amy says.

And Linda, in her minty green scrubs, kneels down in the purple asters at the base of the widening cave and puts her gigantic palms face up as if receiving grace or mercy. And the first baby's head lands in her hands, and she pulls it toward her, out of the cave that shows glimpses of black, starry space around the edges of the infant. The child, who is covered in stardust, whose heart pulsates like the northern lights, looks up at Linda and smiles before standing and flying away, out over the green sea. Within seconds, there is another baby to be delivered. And then another. And another. All of them covered in oily, iridescent galaxies—joyous, right there, in her hands.

Linda can remember a time when motherhood was like directing a string quartet, with Molly and Hope on violin, their candy-red tongues sticking out to the sides in concerted effort. With Bradley on the viola, his eyes closed as if sunbathing. With Rick on the cello, his broad swipes of the bow indicative of his pride, him winking at her as she kept the time for everyone: shoes and socks and retainer cases, fresh fruit consumed and flag football flags remembered and tutus fluffed and small egos defended in the face of bullies and C pluses and pediatricians who insisted there was no need for chest X-rays when, yes, I beg your pardon there absolutely is! Says who? says the doctor. Says me, says Linda. And see? See how she had saved them all from pneumonia? Remember that? That victory? Does anyone remember those days when the director had been allowed to boss around baby doctors and hold the hands or touch the braids or brush the cheeks of the musicians? Does anyone remember that besides Linda?

Linda jolts awake, paralyzed and gaping. She feels the opposite of giant, the flip side of necessary. When the movement returns to her extremities, Linda sits up on the edge of the bed and looks at her bedroom window where the night is turning teal with dawn. She has a sudden urge to insist everyone skip school and work. A pressing need to load the five of them in the car to drive past the airport as a family and count incoming jetliners, an overwhelming urge to cook a big pot of something that impresses and silences everyone. Linda wants to spend the afternoon braiding, not hair, not barrettes, but Hope and Molly and Bradley and Rick into a plait that they cannot escape. She wants to hang them in the kitchen, like a mat of dried onions. She wants them to be still, to be stuck, to be unable to do anything but listen to her old stories, to grasp her eternal devotion, her sacrifices, her suppressed anger. She wants to put them in a place where they are forced to understand her reasons for living and loving and leaving.

Linda eats the remaining buffalo crab bites for lunch and crawls into bed at noon. Dana and Amy are waiting for her.

"A final surge of the littlest babies," Amy explains. "The misses. The almost-were."

"And then the big-hearts and the broken-hearts," Dana says.

"What does that mean?" Linda asks.

"You'll see," Dana says.

Linda and Amy and Dana walk to the blue-shadowed snow-field. Linda wonders what Dana's quiver is for. She has yet to see her draw an arrow other than to wave one or poke one as a warning.

"If you have a question," Dana says. "You might as well ask it before I answer it."

"Well?" Linda says.

"I only shoot in emergencies," Dana says. "Or to do this." She draws her bow and points it at a mountainside. The arrow arcs and lands, piercing the granite. A milky geyser pours forth. "Eggnog anyone?" Dana smiles.

At the portal, the littlest babies are numerous, they pour into Linda's hands by the hundreds, like wet pebbles through her fingers. She is ecstatic, covered in stardust up to her elbows. Then a pause.

"What next?" she asks.

"Look," say Amy and Dana.

Through the opening is a genderless, faceless, line of figures, ordered from the biggest hearts to broken-est hearts to the smallest hearts. Linda strains to see as far as she can. She cannot see the end of the line, but she can tell that the farthest figures appear to have no hearts at all.

"Are you ready?" Amy asks.

"Because this gets more interesting," Dana says.

The first one spills into Linda's arms, easily, more slender than a baby, and then they stand, turning from diseased to robust. The next from wounded to well. The one after that from lethargic to enlivened. After the big-hearts, the broken-hearts arrive. They tell Linda what destroyed them—*the murder, the divorce, the abuse, the guilt*—before they shift and shine and run out to the snowfields laughing, now gods and antelopes and butterflies. Then unexpectedly, after a final broken-heart, the portal abruptly closes. At once, the keyhole is pinched shut on spying, on deliverance.

"Wait," Linda says. "What about the tiny hearts? What about the heartless?"

Amy shakes her head. "Not today."

Dana shrugs. "Better luck next time."

Out on the snowfields are circles of pink pulsing figures, gazelles, snowshoe hares, cockatoos, giraffes, crocuses, an eggnog geyser. The sun is as warm as the tropics, but the snow is unaffected. "Is my work here done?" Linda asks sadly.

"Do you want it to be?" Amy asks.

"No," Linda shakes her head. "But . . ."

"But what?" presses Dana.

Linda takes off running in a madcap way, as if pursued by a cloud of hornets. Where she's going, she doesn't know. Where is the door out of North Colorado? She thinks of Molly and Hope and Bradley and Rick. Of their faces bent over screens, of how dark and repetitive her mornings are, of their persistence in going untouched and their insistence on touching her, of their unimpressed hazel eyes, the intoxicating humid smell of their hair. She darts in zigs and zags—stay, return, withdraw, unite. And then, Linda is down. Felled like a deer. Shot between the shoulder blades with one of Dana's golden arrows, and she can hear Amy and Dana laughing their lusty, defeating roars that call in the rainbow birds and their sky show.

"You didn't think you'd get away that easy, now, did you, cupcake?" Dana shouts.

Amy comes and stands over Linda, blocking the sun. "Why all the fuss, Linda? Hair accessories?"

Linda winces as Dana pulls the arrow from her back, though it doesn't hurt at all. Near the horizon, she sees again the apparitions she saw on her inaugural visit: a unicorn, James Gandolfini, Linda's dead aunt Joan? (Linda's dead aunt Joan!), Charlotte Brontë, a harp seal. She thinks of the trip she was planning for the kids and Rick. South Dakota. Wall Drug. Mount Rushmore. Devils Tower. The trip that no one wanted to go on but her. She thinks of her composting lecture. Of the little bucket of apple cores that only she remembers. She braids the final onion into the mat and hangs it in her mind. "Am I dead?" Linda asks, feeling more alive than ever before.

Amy snorts. "Oh, please," she says, her baton releasing a celebratory confetti storm of rose petals and green scarabs and tadpoles that wriggle down into the snow. "You can do better than that."

Linda thinks. "Can I make a phone call, then?"

Amy and Dana look at one another in wordless consultation. "I suppose," says Amy.

"Just one," says Dana.

Linda takes a moment to consider her options. She could call Rick, to tell him how the washer works. Or the home voicemail, to sing "You Are My Sunshine." There's her estranged brother who probably deserves an apology. And DeeDee Sykes, without whom none of this would have been possible. Finally, Linda decides. She looks out over the snow for a conch shell until Dana rolls her eyes in exasperation and produces one from a fringed pocket. Linda holds it to her ear and waits. "Brenda? Brenda Brock?" she eventually says, sighing. "I just wanted you to know you were right. Right on the money."

When Linda doesn't show up for afternoon carpool, the school calls Rick to come and get Hope and Molly and Bradley. Back at the house, they search for their mother, their wife (their meal-maker, the director of their string quartet, the queen of spangled jeans), starting with the garage where the minivan's open rear hatch reveals four plastic grocery bags of canned Dungeness crab. In the kitchen they see a plate in the sink with six greasy marks, on the table forty finished barrettes (school colors, green and gold, *Go Jaguars!*), thirty unfinished in black and crimson (*Go Stallions!*). They throw back shower curtains and window curtains. They open closets, even drawers. In the bedroom, Linda's phone alarm plays Marimba, but Linda isn't there. Bradley touches her pillow. Molly chokes back tears. Rick turns off the alarm. Hope points to the bedspread, folded halfway back and bulbous. She's afraid to pull it back, so Rick does, fast, the old tablecloth trick. And there it is.

"What is it?" Bradley asks. "What is THAT?"

Hope puts her hand on the shell. It's the size of a tractor tire, a baby pool. Where the top half and bottom half meet, there's a cobalt mantle, a ruffle of shimmering tissue.

"It's an oyster," Hope says.

"A mussel," Molly says.

"A mollusk," Rick adds.

Bradley pushes in front of them all and places his hands on

either side of the giant clam's blue frill.

"It looks like it's smiling," Molly says.

"I'm going to open it," says Bradley.

And he does. He pries the top from the bottom and the bottom from the top until the shell has opened wide to reveal its insides for all to see.

"A pearl," Hope gasps.

"A pearl," Molly repeats.

And they lean together, the four of them to stare. Inside of the giant clam rests a pearl the size of a schoolhouse globe. It gleams bright and white and rainbowed, and when they stare into it, it reflects their faces back to them. Not the faces they see in the mirror but faces that are flawless and loved. Faces of who they are to Linda and who they might be, one day, to themselves.

Faster

It was 1987. Everyone Dominick knew was gorging, engorged, gorgeous. There was finally enough money. People could buy the tap shoes, the electric toothbrushes, the giant faux-wood microwaves big enough to hold Butterballs. They could afford a year's supply of the old red Doritos and the new blue Doritos and the old Coke and the new Coke and coke, uncapitalized. Everyone capitalized. They could have the Guess denim vest, the Ralph Lauren dress, the best of the best.

Dominick quit eating at 5:55 p.m. on January one of that rich year. It was an unplanned resolution. Dominick's mother came to the table wearing an entire bottle of Giorgio. His sister, Danielle, an entire can of Aqua Net. Inside his father was a fifth of Smirnoff. Dominick could hear the vodka slosh as his father pulled up his chair. Dominick imagined a little yacht in his father's stomach, going back and forth on the waves. On that little yacht, Dominick imagined tiny people—also drunk—with even tinier yachts going back and forth inside of them.

At dinner, there was no blessing, merely a toast. *To wealth*, his mother said. *To wealth*, everyone but Dominick answered. Dominick ate a single black-eyed pea off his plate. The plate was rimmed with gold stirrups as if his family rode horses (which they didn't) or owned them (which they could have). *Eat, eat*, his family said. *Fast, fast*, Dominick thought. The way he saw it, the less he consumed, the faster the world was saved. Dominick was madly in love with the idea of saving. No one he knew was saved or saving. Everyone he knew was spent or spending. Inside of Dominick, the lone pea rattled like a penny in a beggar's coffee can.

Dominick was twelve and gaunt and downy-haired, everywhere. His pediatrician had just returned from a worldwide medical meeting in the Netherlands. He now knew everything there was to know about anorexia and was buying none of it.

"He's not anorexic," the doctor said. "He's besieged by *Weltschmerz*!" This was the German word for "ho-hum." "Right now, the boy has little appetite for food because he has little appetite for life," the doctor told Dominick's mother. "Give him a year. Next thing you know he'll be all about sex and steaks."

Dominick knew this was baloney, because he could think of baloney and say "baloney" without craving baloney. Dominick's mother, however, breathed a sigh of relief. She smoothed her silk scarf. The scarf was covered with saddles and riding crops. In the real world, Dominick's mother was terrified of everything equine, miniature ponies included.

By February, the only things Dominick had consumed were a

bag of red Doritos, a bag of blue Doritos, and several items that he cataloged on a piece of paper: three silver-dollar pancakes, seven M&Ms, one tin of sardines, four cheese cubes, two shelled sunflower seeds.

On Valentine's Day, Dominick fell in love with something new, something in addition to saving. He fell in love with the idea of eating things that people would not think to eat: a single piece of uncooked fettuccine licked and dipped into powdered Tang. A pinch of fish food. Gray-pink erasers from worn pencils. Limp pickles from a Quarter Pounder, left to grow cold on the Mercedes dashboard between errands.

As Dominick disappeared, he appeared. Now, he could see a visible pulse in his wrist and abdomen and ankle. There were new tendons behind his knees and on the tops of his feet. Here, at last, were his cheekbones and hip bones and eye sockets. Without food, his mind grew dim but his desires became clear: want nothing, take nothing, be nothing. Save everything.

Meanwhile, people went to the mall. The mall expanded. The people expanded. Wallets expanded, overnight, like dough rising under dish towels. Children across the ocean stacked denim six stories high. They pulled levers, and the levers cut out blue jeans like cookies. The children stitched zippers and sewed rhinestones. They sent the blue jeans across the sea to America on weighty barges. They were paid in coins. Their hands bled. Who would consume all of the jeans? At home, Dominick lay on the couch and ran his bony fingers over his ribcage, strumming himself like a harp.

A new doctor said that if Dominick didn't eat, there would be no choice but to insert a feeding tube. The doctor told Dominick's mother to put one broccoli floret and one chicken nugget on a blue plate and present it to Dominick. If he did not eat them in thirty minutes, he was to be sent to his room for an additional thirty minutes, after which the floret and nugget were to be reintroduced on a red plate. Dominick and his mother played this game for eight hours, during which time Dominick ate nothing and his mother drank everything. While in his room, Dominick stared at his white walls and had visions. He saw monks eating monkeys eating bananas. The bananas were prophetic. One banana peeled itself and out came a scroll. Unrolled, it said: *KEEP UP THE GOOD WORK.*

The day before the feeding tube, Dominick's father took him to the circus. His father had one fifth of Smirnoff inside of him and another inside his coat. He pushed Dominick in a wheelchair in silence. In the circus's center ring, Dominick watched an impassive tiger walk on its hind legs, a gloomy brown bear pedal a tricycle. Then came a man in a red leotard with a mustache like a soaring blackbird. He brought out three shining swords and—one, two, three!—they went down his throat. The audience roared and—one, two, three!—the swords came out. The tiger growled. The bear growled. Dominick's stomach growled.

That night, Dominick went into the pantry. On the top shelf he found a little netted bag of chocolate coins. He brought them down and removed their copper wrappers and ate them all. They landed inside of him like pennies in a beggar's coffee can. His mother and father and sister, Danielle, took three separate cars to three different candy stores and bought bag after netted bag of chocolate coins. At home, they piled the coins in front of Dominick. Some were gold, some were silver, some were copper.

Dominick ate them all. The next day—and the day after that, and the day after that—his family went out and bought chocolate money with real money and Dominick ate everything put before him. Before long, Dominick's face filled out and his tendons went into hiding and his pulse could no longer be felt under his fat. Now, the way he saw it, the faster he consumed, the faster the world was saved. And the faster the world was saved, the more there was for Dominick to love. The more of Dominick there was to love.

Lush

Sawyer is seven. For three straight mornings in Boca, she cracks the door of the bathroom between her pink room and the blue one where her half brother Charles and his college girlfriend Judith are sleeping. She eases the door open a slow, single inch. It is spring break. Her parents have rented a beach-front house laden with white wicker. They're bankers.

"We went to Woodstock before Wall Street," Sawyer's father says to Judith at dinner on the night they arrive. They've served Judith crab claws she does not know how to manage. "You and Charles can share a room."

"It's a twin," Sawyer's mother says. "You'll have to get creative."

This and the crab make Judith blush. Charles keeps on eating, voracious and shiny, butter all over his face and hands. Sawyer holds up a crab claw and cracks it for Judith, to show her how it's done.

Sawyer has a new plastic pony the color of grape gum. His name is Morrison. On the first morning of vacation, Sawyer gets up at eight and sits on the bathmat near the toilet, raking through Morrison's mane and tail with a comb. Behind the closed door, Sawyer's brother is breathing hard. Sawyer grooms her pony. She braids his tail, fastens it with a barrette. After a while, the panting stops. There's not a sound from Judith. Sawyer counts backwards from 300 Mississippi, then opens the door and takes a peek. There's Judith, flat on her stomach in the far twin bed. Charles is asleep on her back, his bare bottom the color of snow. Judith is trapped beneath him, but awake, the bedsheet drawn to her middle. She gives Sawyer a little smile and a four-finger wave. She seems sorry.

Judith has a tattoo of a cross on the back of her neck, which is revealed when she wears a ponytail. Charles calls her "a Jesus freak." Judith has a big laugh to make up for the fact that she often appears to be on the verge of tears. Around the pool, she wears a yellow bikini and has poor posture. Charles says that for the size of Judith's ass, you'd think her tits would be bigger. Sawyer hears her brother announce this into the cordless phone, over and over. "For the size of her ass, you'd think her tits would be bigger."

Judith comes from South Dakota. Sawyer's family comes from Westchester and can take a train into the city to see *Les Mis* whenever they want. "I only know corn!" Judith jokes. She looks out of place everywhere, which makes her seem young and foolish, and that's why Sawyer likes her. She's like a new classmate that Sawyer feels sorry for.

On the second morning, when Judith wakes up, she sees Sawyer's hazel eye in the door crack, just like yesterday. What has Sawyer heard? Not Judith, that's for sure. The wicker headboard is noisy. Charles is noisy. But Judith is silent. If she's going to be bad, she can at least be quiet. She can at least put her face in the pillow and name things from the Bible that begin with J: Jesus, Jerusalem, Jezebel, Judith. Of course, she suspects this is sacrilegious, but at this point, what isn't? She's letting Charles go right in the door that won't get her pregnant but will definitely send her to Hell. There's no redemption now. When all the other girls in the dorm got tattoos of snakes, Judith got the cross, and what did that accomplish? Judith glances around the room. There's an empty wine bottle by the bedside, a washcloth on the floor, a bra on display. She flutters her fingers in another sheepish wave and smiles her apologetic smile.

That night, Judith remembers to slide the empty wine bottle under the bed and put her bra under her pillow. At 7:30 in the morning, when Charles rolls her over on her stomach, she says, "Wait." She gets up and tries to lock the bathroom door, but it won't lock from their side. Still, the show goes on. The whole time Charles is on her back, Judith watches the door, waiting for that hazel eye. When Charles slumps off to sleep, Judith crawls out from under him. She puts on a baggy sweatshirt and clean underwear. She sits on the other bed and waits for Sawyer.

In the morning, Sawyer opens the door to find Judith sitting on the nearby twin in a sweatshirt, smiling. She invites her into the bathroom to have a look at Morrison.

"Morrison is going to a horse show," she says. "It's in West Palm, and he has to compete with Queen Elizabeth's champion."

"What's his name?" Judith asks, pressing her palms to her temples.

"I just told you," Sawyer huffs. "Morrison."

"No," Judith says. "The Queen's horse."

"Oh," Sawyer says. "You mean *her*. Lady Marmalade the Fourth."

Judith shakes three aspirin out of a pill bottle. "I don't like competition. It scares me." She jiggles the tablets in her hand like dice.

Sawyer frowns as Judith drinks from a toy cup. "Have you seen the closet in my room?" she asks. "I've made it into an elevator that goes to Planet Popsicle."

Judith squints and swallows. "I have not had the pleasure."

"Well, come and see," Sawyer says.

Judith crawls into the closet on her hands and knees. The door is slatted, and the tropical morning sun stripes the walls light and dark pink. The closet smells of watered-down little-girl perfume, the sort that comes packaged with make-believe compacts and cheap, glittery nail polish that peels off like glue. When Judith sniffs the air, she can remember when God loved her—back when she made straight As and was going to stay in South Dakota and be a weathergirl. Back when achievement—competition—had tricked her into a sense of security. Her plan back then had been to have good highlights and three children who weren't afraid of cows. But then, in Judith's sophomore year of high school, her mother died of breast cancer. In her junior year, Judith entered the "Big Dreams" essay contest to make her dead mother proud.

She wrote something cliché about a silo and the Empire State Building. Something about tractors, taxis. Something about preciousness and the present moment. And the next thing Judith knew, she was in Times Square, then crying in a city dorm, then drinking too much beer, snorting cocaine, getting a tattoo, and taking Ritalin and Xanax. And then Charles.

"Do you want cake?" Sawyer asks. "I made it yesterday." She opens a toy oven and brings out a little silver heart-shaped pan filled with old, flat, yellow cake.

Always eat the cake, Judith's mother liked to say.

"Yes, I'll have some cake," Judith says.

Sawyer flips the yellow heart out of the pan, into her own palm. She tears it in half and hands one side to Judith. "Charles's mother was a lush," she says. "Daddy left her when Charles was ten and they never saw her again. She drank with breakfast. She drank at lunch and dinner. One time she drove right into a dry cleaner's and Charles bit through his tongue."

Judith swallows the cake. It tastes like salt and metal. "That can't be right," Judith says. "Charles told me his mother was dead, like mine. That she died of breast cancer, too."

Sawyer shrugs. "He lies."

"Who lies about something like that?" Judith says. "You must have the story wrong."

"You can ask my dad. But I wouldn't if I were you."

The aspirin and cake feel stuck in Judith's throat. Charles told her the story at freshman orientation. They'd been asked to find three things in common. They both liked mushroom pizza. They were both bad at karaoke and loved it anyway. They both had dead mothers.

"Is she still alive?" Judith asks.

"I hope not," Sawyer says.

"What was her name?" Judith asks.

"Lucinda," Sawyer says. "Lucinda the lush."

Judith says it to herself. She sees the dry cleaner's window, Charles's bleeding mouth. She wonders if the woman has maybe changed her name, remarried, been in and out of rehab.

"Elevator closing," Sawyer announces. "Ready for liftoff?"

On the fourth night, Sawyer can hear Charles and Judith arguing. It's mostly Judith doing the talking.

"What else have you lied to me about?" Judith asks. "Have there been other girls?"

Sawyer does not hear Charles answer. There's some fumbling and scraping. A long sniff. "Have a line," her brother says.

"You didn't answer my questions, Charles." Judith's voice is getting louder and higher. She sounds like someone who's lost something. Sawyer remembers a lady in the park: *Have you seen my dog? He's everything to me.* Judith's voice trembles the same way. "Answer me! Is your mother alive? Have there been other girls? This isn't even coke. What are you getting me into?"

There's a pause. More scraping and shuffling. Another long sniff, then nothing for a long time. Sawyer hears a sob from Judith.

"I know you think I'm stupid. You think I'm fat. You think corn is dumb. Well, who makes your food, Charles? Where do you think bacon and eggs come from? A window box?"

Sawyer is nervous. She puts Morrison under the bathroom sink. She sits on the bathmat, on her hands.

"I used to be a good person," Judith says. "I used to know who I was and what I wanted, and then I met you and now I don't fit in anywhere. I'm too smart for South Dakota and too stupid for New York. Where do I go? Besides Hell. Answer me that, Charles. Where do I go besides Hell?"

Sawyer hears more sobs. Then a smack, a yelp, a groan. "I want my mother!" Judith cries. "Jericho, Joseph, Jesus!"

Charles finally joins in. "Jesus is right! You've really lost your mind this time."

Sawyer hears a scuffle. The sound of sheets being torn from a bed. Sawyer wonders, should she look? Just a little? She goes to the door and opens it a crack. Her eye sees what it sees: her brother's fist raised over Judith, and Judith, cowering on the ground, her arms making a cross over her face. Sawyer shuts the door. She goes into her closet with Morrison. The elevator goes up, up, up to where the popsicles are.

Judith wakes from a fitful sleep. Her nose has bled and dried. If Charles weren't on her back, she'd get up, pack her things, thumb a ride to a Waffle House or a bus station. But Charles is heavy. She goes in and out of sleep, or consciousness. She dreams of thirst. Of being on a bridge over a rushing river. She has no bucket, only a rope that she dangles in the current and hauls up to press to her lips.

When she wakes again, Charles is gone. There is blood on the pillowcase that has soaked through to the pillow itself. She sits up with some effort. The room is blue and bright. The house is silent. She goes into the bathroom, holding the pillow. Her face, from the nose down, is red with dried blood, her right nostril nearly crusted shut.

"My brother did that, didn't he."

Judith startles. In the mirror, at her side, is Sawyer holding Morrison.

"Everyone went to play golf," Sawyer says. "I told them I'd stay. That you would babysit me when you woke up."

Judith remembers the dream: the thirst, the rope. "There were seven devils in Mary Magdalene," she says.

"Who's that?" Sawyer asks.

"A girl I know," Judith says.

"Who were they?"

"Who were who?"

"The seven devils."

Judith washes her face, slowly, with handfuls of water. "I don't know," she says. "I shouldn't have brought it up."

Sawyer helps Judith wash the pillowcase and pillow. They lay them out to dry on a chaise by the pool. Sawyer puts on a bathing suit printed with daisies, and she floats in an inner tube, humming, in the shallow end. Judith sits in a chaise with a glass of orange juice and vodka, wearing sunglasses. "Coke," she eventually says. "Pills, booze, Charles, ink, crab, cancer. There're your seven devils. There you go."

Sawyer twirls her legs underwater and spins in a circle. "Everybody gets bloody noses," she says. "A boy in my class gets them twice a week and he's still a good person."

"Oh, is he?" Judith finishes her drink. "Well, good for him."

After that, Judith doesn't have much to say. Sawyer knows better than to suggest hide-and-seek or Marco Polo. When the sun gets hot, they go inside and watch television on the couch. The coyote's wearing roller skates with rockets. He is forever doomed but never dead.

Judith goes in and out of sleep. When she wakes up for real, she says, "Hey. What about some popsicles?"

Feeling a sudden lurch of joy, Sawyer goes to the freezer and brings out a double orange popsicle and snaps it in two. Sawyer eats one half and Judith eats the other.

"That bubble gum perfume of yours," Judith says. "Could you go get it and put it on my neck?"

That night, Sawyer doesn't hear fighting. She doesn't hear talking or breathing or slapping or sniffing. She sits on the bathmat with Morrison until she gives up and goes to bed. The next morning, when she tries to spy, her bathroom door is locked. When she presses her ear to it, she can't hear a thing. In the kitchen, her parents and Charles are around the white wicker dining table.

"Judith is going home early," her mother says, smiling.

Her father is smiling, too. "I think she's had all the fun she's going to have."

Charles hunches over a plate of eggs and eats ravenously. Sawyer's mother brings Sawyer a blueberry muffin on a cocktail napkin. When she's finished, her mother takes her out of the house. They get in one of the rental cars and drive around until they find an old Kmart, where Sawyer's mother buys her another plastic pony, this one the color of an orange popsicle. Back at the house, in the bathroom, Sawyer finds that Judith has left behind her toothbrush, a hair elastic, and an old razor. Morrison is on the counter, his hooves on a scrap of notebook paper: *Thanks for everything, popsicle pal!*

Sawyer picks up Morrison and goes out to the pool. Her parents recline on chaises, side by side. They're holding drinks, wearing sunglasses. Sawyer cannot see their eyes.

"I want to ride horses," Sawyer says.

"Right this second?" Her father sighs. "Or generally speaking?"

"I want to learn how to ride them in shows."

"Well," her mother says, taking a sip of her drink, "we can think about it. That kind of riding is very competitive."

Sawyer holds up Morrison so they can see how well groomed he is. "I like competition. Competition doesn't scare me."

The Split

hey ended their marriage to save their marriage.

"If we stay in this any longer," she said, "it's going to fail."

He saw it differently, which was no surprise.

"The only way to stop failing," he said, "is to get out."

They decided to break up over dinner at a restaurant they'd frequented when they were dating. They'd forgotten about the restaurant until they reached the impasse, then it just fondly reappeared as an option, like a recipe fallen from a soft cookbook.

"How about Gerald's?" she said. "For steaks?"

"Gerald's," he repeated thoughtfully, with a glint in his eyes that signified either sadness or glee, "for seafood."

So, Gerald's it was. In the parking lot, they held hands as they walked from the car to the restaurant door, which he held open for her and at which she smiled, because there were no hard feelings, only differences. It was cold outside and her hand was soft and icy and his was damp and warm and the autumn sky was the color of gravestones. The restaurant put off the smell of woodsmoke, which made her think of Christmas and reminded him of hunting ducks. Once inside, they sat in a far corner of the restaurant in a black leather booth as shiny as motor oil.

"We could split something," she suggested, eyeing the menu, though as soon as the words were out of her mouth, she knew it was a silly thing to say. He wouldn't want half of a petite filet and there was no easy way to share a bowl of bouillabaisse.

"Or we could just split," he said with a little laugh. The play on words was both tender and pitiful, like a child's cough. They both fell silent in a way that was best overcome with a toast. "To Gerald's," he said, raising his martini.

"Then and now," she said with champagne.

All who knew them were bewildered by their decision.

"It was going to fail anyway," she explained.

"Then wait till it fails," her friends said.

"It didn't seem broken," his friends said.

"Get the plane on the ground while you still have an engine," he replied.

They went to a therapist so they could say they'd tried everything. The therapist held up a series of inkblot cards.

"An Easter lily," she said.

"An appendicitis," he said.

"Joan of Arc," she said.

"A rack of lamb," he said.

"Two moths kissing," she said.

"An airbag, deployed," he said.

The therapist confirmed what they already knew. They went home to divide their things, but instead of dividing them, they sat on the back porch in their coats and didn't speak. He claimed the view of the thin crescent moon as his, while she went on thinking the thoughts she had never shared. After some time, a speck of something fell into her right eye, and she blinked and blinked, then stood and said, "Something has fallen into my right eye."

He looked at her for a moment as if he still loved her and said, "Let me help you with that."

Inside, she tilted her head back and held her eye open with her thumb and forefinger, while he stared deep into an eye he had once stared deeply into. "I don't see anything," he said.

"But I can feel something," she said.

She rinsed her face and her eyes at the kitchen sink, and when she was done, she looked like a child who had finished crying about something adults didn't think was worth crying over. She went into their bedroom and got under the covers on her side of the bed, and he followed her and got on top of the covers on his side of the bed. They lay on their backs and stared at the ceiling and held hands right down the center. Before long, they slept.

That night, they both dreamed the same dream. That her right eye watered and watered until it made a swift, black river that carried both of them away. For a while, the current kept them in sight of one another, but eventually, they lost track of each other and all either of them could see was the river pouring out in front of them like ink and something bright and pink bobbing, in the distance, on the horizon. Neither could say for sure if it was the head of the other or the sun coming up or the sun going down, but one thing was certain: they were finally getting somewhere.

April

April had never baked a pie for someone she knew, much less someone she had never met, and yet here she was on a Saturday morning in July, in a stiff apron that still bore its price tag, cubing cold butter. Her blind date was driving seventy miles east for dinner and seventy miles back, with no chance of sex. She had intentionally shaved everywhere but there. There was dog hair on the bedsheets. The bedsheets were flannel. The heat index was as high as the chickenpox fever April had run as a child, when she'd hallucinated her grandmother, in a hoop-skirt, carrying a scythe. April knew nothing of the blind date other than he worked with numbers, that he sometimes played crossminton, which April had had to Google: *What crossminton?* Still, he was traveling an hour, both ways, to break bread with a stranger. It was courageous. Maniacal, even. Dessert seemed an appropriate stipend.

April sent pictures of the unbaked raspberry to her friend Kendra, who was defiantly single.

A PIE? Kendra texted. *DO YOU EVEN VOTE?*

April slid the pie into the oven and sat down to watch it, sure it would combust.

SO CHURCH OF YOU! Kendra went on. *BUT ALSO SLUT.*

April was without shame. She'd been lonely for eighteen months and done everything suggested to amend it. For starters, she'd purchased a journal. A bismuth-pink diary embossed with *I LOVE ME!*, in which she had scribbled *i love me!* 6,446 times, only to learn that she did love herself, very much in fact, but only as a friend.

Then, she'd gone alone to Miami and sat on the beach in an oversized Dolphins sweatshirt. She hated football. She had not packed appropriately. Was anything colder than 60 in Florida? *Spend the time meditating,* her family had said, but meditating felt as terrible as chicken stuck between molars, so April spent the four days contemplating the amount of tampon applicators and sea sponges washed ashore. The applicators must have been from cruise ships. The sea sponges must have been trying to escape the applicators. April noted that the sponges were remarkable in their confidence and innovation. They did not resemble harmless yellow dinner rolls. These were suggestive squirrel-colored anomalies shaped like exhaust pipes, toddlers' forearms, linked bratwursts.

On the final day, April took a Hefty bag to the beach and filled it with sponges. In the hotel, she pressed the Hefty bag free of air and put it in her checked luggage. Her plan was to bleach the sponges and use them as décor, conversation pieces. *These are from the meditation retreat I took in Miami.* But upon unpacking, the stench was so horrendous the sponges went straight into the garbage bin, which went straight to the curb.

That first night back, April watched the bin from her kitchen window. Around midnight, the neighborhood raccoons climbed inside and got ahold of the sponges, but even they were appalled. They dragged the sponges up and down the street, frantically, as if the sponges were chasing them, attached to them. In the morning, April saw: Dade County intestines strewn every which way. Buzzards alighted, screeched, lurched backward. None of it brought April any closer to companionship, but for a short time it did distract her from her solitude. *Miami 8.2/10*, she wrote on the final page of her pink journal.

Next, a cousin sent April a link to a trio of local support groups and April, undaunted, enrolled in all three. The first group—Lover's Leap—consisted of young women, all with fresh diamond solitaires on their left hands. They met at a SpringHill Suites, in a small conference room that smelled of instant oatmeal and chlorine.

"I'm doing a ballerina," one of the girls said. "That way I can dance without tripping."

"You don't want that," said another girl, whose eyelashes were like tarantulas. "What you want is fingertip."

"Mantilla," said another girl, monotone. "Weirdly hot."

April broke in. "I'm sorry. What are we talking about?"

The girls turned to consider April as if they had just noticed a German shepherd in their midst. "Wedding veils," said Tarantula Eyes. "You have any opinion on wedding veils?"

"Well, no," April shrugged. "I came to talk about love. Or leaping. That's the theme here, right?" This time, the girls looked at April as if she'd lifted her shirt to show them a keloid scar. "Hey," she said. "I just thought of something that people who are leaping into love and people who are heartbroken have in common. Actually, two things. Neither can eat or sleep."

"Can't eat?" one girl said. "I wish."

"Here's a reason I can't sleep," Tarantula Eyes said. "Guest lists."

"Or what song we should dance to," said another. She was unnaturally suntanned, almost the color of barbecue sauce.

"Yes," two girls groaned in a way that sounded sexual. "That."

Shortly thereafter, April got up. She walked right out of Lover's Leap and no one even noticed. By then, they were debating how miniature a crab cake had to be to be considered miniature.

The second support group—Long-Term Love—was held in a humid fellowship hall crammed with women in their seventies, all of whom were caregivers for husbands they resented. There was much discussion of bedpans and whether squirting Visine into someone's drinking water could actually kill them in a way that was untraceable.

"I hear it works," said a woman named Fran. "Stomach pains and then blammo."

"Report back," said a woman named Doris.

"Yes," said another woman named Doris. "Please do."

April had high hopes for the third support group—Love Survivors. It sounded like something that would involve brass plaques, personal testimonies.

"I will never do monogamy again," April heard a woman by

the decaf dispenser say. The woman wore a spandex dress printed with black and chartreuse stripes. "These are tiger." She ran an acrylic nail down her ribcage. "Not cougar."

"Same," said a woman sniffing an open canister of Coffee Mate. "I'm just here to play backgammon. Maybe get into something weird. Not like a threesome, but like crystals. Have you tried crystals?"

"Oh, yes," said the woman in the tiger dress. "I have a smoky tourmaline inserted vaginally right now."

April considered an imaginary hangnail.

"Did you know there are over forty names for the cougar besides cougar?" the woman dressed as a tiger said.

"Is one of them Tiffany?" the other woman asked, holding out her hand.

After the support groups, April did nothing related to love for a few months. She bought Kirby cucumbers at the farmer's market and made homemade bread-and-butter pickles. She gave three jars to an elderly neighbor who later confessed they made him very ill.

She bought an expandable file folder for things she thought might be related to taxes and labeled it *TAXES*, but somehow only an L.L.Bean catalog ended up in the folder.

She ate peanut butter from a jar for dinner. She used a celery stick as a spoon so there were no dishes.

She said yes to a work trip no one else wanted to say yes to. It was a conference held in Kansas City. The conference was about workplace apathy. It was titled "How to Make People Care." On the flight from Atlanta to Kansas City, a woman next to April talked from buckle to unbuckle.

"You know how I knew my ex was angling to become my ex? There were all sorts of clues. Do you want to know some of them? You should. Because people who want out always give themselves away."

The woman smelled very much like coconuts that were masking something pitiful. Urine, gin. April felt a need to know the ex's name, and then, like magic:

"James would tell me all the time how much his friends hated their wives. He'd say 'Joe says he'd kill Ruth if he could get away with it.' Or: 'Mike is leaving Felicia once her father dies.' At the time, my father was deathly ill. And James did own a gun. He'd gone duck hunting once in our marriage. When he started saying these things, I began to think back on that duck hunting trip. Maybe it had been an excuse to get a gun to later kill me with?"

April was unsure how many times she was required to nod at someone she had not explicitly agreed to listen to.

"One time," the woman said, "James told our kids: 'If your mother and I ever get divorced, I'll always wink at her. If we're at a mutual party, I'll look across the room and wink at her. I'll never *not* wink at her.' Pardon my French, but: What the actual fuck?"

April nodded. When the flight attendant came by, the woman ordered two Coke Zeros and washed down three or four pills the size of Mentos.

"On our fifteenth anniversary, though, it was just curtains. That was when we went to Palm Springs. One night at the hotel, I woke up at one thirty in the morning and he was gone. His side of the bed wasn't even warm. I went down to the lobby looking for him. There were three bars at the hotel; it was big. And the bars were just packed. It was a Groupon weekend, and I had to go bar to bar, in my sweatpants, but finally I see him. He's on a barstool

and there's a woman next to him. Blonde, ponytail. Their backs
are to me, so I sit down at a cocktail table right behind them, and
I can see: he's showing her pictures of our kids—my kids! The
people who came out of my body, and he's saying: 'Have you been
to Glacier National Park? Glacier is God's best work.' Those were
MY words. *God's best work.* The nerve! I sat there for an hour at
the table. A waitress brought me a glass of pinot, but I couldn't
even drink it. Right before I thought about confronting him, an
earthquake hit. Tremors had been happening all weekend, but
this one was a little bigger. Everyone was drunk and just laughed
it off. Some drinks spilled. A woman in heels fell into a potted
plant. But that was my sign. The earthquake. I went back to the
room and pretended to be asleep. He finally came back up two
hours later. What do you think they did, huh? And that was our
anniversary night! You know, I had an engraved gold pen for him
that I ended up putting in the toilet tank. Do you know I stayed
with him for two years after that? I was waiting for my youngest
to turn nine. Third grade seemed better, but honestly first grade
would have been more humane. I wonder if anyone ever found it.
It was worth something, that pen. Maybe a plumber. But what
does a plumber need a gold pen for?"

April was done nodding. Her own marriage had lasted seven
years. Throughout, she'd had a recurring dream that she was on
a sandy stretch of road chasing a tumbleweed. On her first night
as a single woman, she dreamed she finally caught up to the tumbleweed. She spent an eternity under a hot desert sun untangling
it, only to find at its center a dead white mouse. The mouse was
dehydrated, as light as a peanut shell. April shook it, held it to her
ear. She knew its heart was nothing more than a flake of salt even
though she was only going by sound.

"I was the one who had to file," the woman said. She was rushing her story now. The plane was on the ground, almost at the gate. The sound of two hundred seatbelts being released filled the air. Knives on whetstones. "Turns out, he hates being divorced. He looks at me like he needs water. But me? I'm free. It's like I had a lung transplant." The woman took a deep breath as proof. "My advice? Find someone who loves like you, because you're both in the same canoe. If only one of you is paddling, it's just circles."

After that, the woman said nothing. When April saw her again at baggage claim, the woman looked through her like she was a window with a terrible view.

The last thing April had done before agreeing to the blind date was the consult. She knew it was a horrible idea but thought the procedure might fast-track her to love.

"You can't go wrong with 350s," the surgeon had said. "It's what my wife and everyone in her book club picked."

The surgeon sat, wide-legged and voyeuristic, on an examination stool, while April stood sideways in front of the mirror. She bent down, bent over. She tried to imagine a man she did not yet know, his head on her ample chest, washed ashore and smitten. At one point, the surgeon crossed his legs and revealed a pair of baby blue, monogrammed socks. *WTA*, they announced. *What the actual,* April thought. After some time, he stood up and came over to April. He put his insured hands down inside the clinical jog bra like he owned it, which he did, and he shuffled the loose implants until his face reflected satisfaction.

"It's a mystery book club," he said. "But I'm not sure they ever figure anything out. Maybe you'd like to join?"

April imagined a room full of women with pretend breasts stumped by pretend murders pretending they knew how to live a decent life. Before she left the consultation, the doctor showed April a medical device, a funnel of sorts, a clinical icing bag. He demonstrated how the implants would slide into the funnel and under April's pectorals "like custard into an éclair. Easy as pie."

In the parking lot, April sat numb in her running car. She saw two silicone mounds hermetically sealed in one of the surgeon's dark closets. A pair of crystal balls. If she fell in love, would she run faster toward them or away from them? April shifted into reverse, her phone rang, and she shifted back into park. It was a friend, not Kendra, with the name of a man. *He has it together* was all the friend said, as if that were enough, and after ten days of wavering, April decided it was. That had been two weeks ago, and now, here she was, in a stiff apron, watching a pie change from anemic to jaundiced.

April's phone dinged. Kendra.

PIES FALL APART. A CAKE HAS SUBSTANCE AT LEAST!

i had cake at my wedding, April typed. *it had a pvc pipe down the center of it for stability and guess what still collapsed?*

THE MARRIAGE? Kendra responded.

April looked at her watch. It was small and platinum and she had bought it for herself, but she did not like it. In twenty minutes, the pie would be ready. In two hours, she would be. In five years, when asked when it was exactly that she had fallen in love, April would have to stop and think. Had there been a specific moment? Was it when he had climbed the porch stairs two at a time to meet her? Was it how his face had lit up even though she had not been holding out a pie, but his face had acted

235

as if she were? Was it when he'd said: *You're exactly what I've been looking for. Wait. That came out wrong. You're exactly what I thought you might be. Wait. That was also wrong.* Or was it when she'd said her silent thoughts aloud and hadn't scared him off? *How was the drive? I'm glad you're here. The day is almost over, and I've been waiting for it to start. Because somewhere out there, things that are not from the sea are washing ashore and depressing someone who has saved for years to be on that shore and see only sea-things.* Or maybe it was when she'd shown him her kitchen and gestured to the pie. Maybe it was when, after dinner, they had gone into the kitchen together and cut into the pie together and stared, together, as the pie fell apart. Maybe it had been then. When everything on the inside turned into everything on the outside.

Acknowledgments

I am beyond grateful for Sarabande Books and its dream team: Kristen Renee Miller, Joanna Englert, Danika Isdahl, Natalie Wollenzien, Sam Hall, and Emma Aprile; for generous authors Andrew Bertaina, Jen Fawkes, Hannah Pittard, Karen Tucker, and Dana Vachon; for the support of *AGNI*, *American Short Fiction*, *Grist*, the *Idaho Review*, *Shenandoah*, *The Best American Short Stories*, *The Best Small Fictions*, Catapult, and Fractured Lit; and for the many special souls in my circle, particularly: my sister, my sisters.

The stories in this collection previously appeared/will appear in the following publications:

New Ohio Review, "Red Flags"

Laurel Review, "Rocks 4 Sale"

Gulf Coast, "Wild Child"

Quarter After Eight, "The Joneses"
    (previously "Meet the Joneses")

American Short Fiction, "Ricky," winner of the 2020
    American Short(er) Fiction Prize

Grist, "Cray," winner of the 2021 ProForma Contest

Moon City Review, "Dawn"

Juked, "Nine Dreams about Marriage"

Permafrost, "Love Blue"

The Greensboro Review, "I'm Your Venus"

Slice, "Ingrid" (previously "Inconceivable")

Raleigh Review, "The Yardstick" (previously "Yardstick")

NELLE, "Beans"

TRNSFR, "Threesome"

The Chattahoochee Review, "Petal"

Idaho Review, "The Wind" (previously "Windy")

Fractured Lit Anthology 3, "Brain, Brian"

Catapult's *Tiny Nightmares: Very Short Tales of Horror*,
     "The Owner"

Lumina, "North Colorado" (previously "Shell Game")

Shenandoah and *The Best Small Fictions 2022*, "Faster"

AGNI, "Lush," Distinguished Story, *The Best American
     Short Stories 2022*

Good River Review, "The Split"

Indiana Review, "April" (previously "Pie")

Whitney Collins is the recipient of a 2020 Pushcart Prize, a 2020 Pushcart Special Mention, a *Best American Short Stories 2022* Distinguished Story, and winner of the 2020 American Short(er) Fiction Prize and the 2021 ProForma Contest. Her stories have appeared in *The Best Small Fictions 2022, Fractured Lit Anthology 3*, and *Tiny Nightmares: Very Short Tales of Horror*, as well as *AGNI, American Short Fiction, Gulf Coast*, and the *Idaho Review*, among others. Whitney's previous story collection, *Big Bad*, won the 2019 Mary McCarthy Prize in Short Fiction, the 2022 Gold Medal IPPY Award for Short Story/Fiction, and the 2021 Bronze Medal INDIES Award for Short Stories. Whitney received her MFA from Spalding University's Naslund-Mann Graduate School of Writing.

Sarabande Books is a nonprofit independent literary press headquartered in Louisville, Kentucky. Established in 1994 to champion poetry, fiction, and essay, we are committed to creating lasting editions that honor exceptional writing. With over two hundred titles in print, we have earned a dedicated readership and a national reputation as a publisher of diverse forms and innovative voices.